Carol Clewlow was born and brought up in Somerset where she trained as a reporter on a weekly paper. She spent three years in Belfast on a local daily paper before leaving to travel in the Middle East and Asia. Her home is now in the North-east of England where she worked for twelve years as a free-lance journalist. *Keeping the Faith* is her first novel. She has also published a second novel, *A Woman's Guide to Adultery*.

KEEPING
THE FAITH

Carol Clewlow

faber and faber

LONDON · BOSTON

First published in 1988
by Faber and Faber Limited
3 Queen Square London WC1N 3AU
This paperback edition first published in 1989

Printed in Great Britain by
Richard Clay Ltd, Bungay, Suffolk
All rights reserved

British Library Cataloguing in Publication Data

Clewlow, Carol
Keeping the faith.
I. Title
823'.914[F]   PR6053.L48/

ISBN 0–571–15292–9

Then shall the Kingdom of Heaven be likened unto ten virgins which took their lamps and went forth to meet the Bridegroom.

And five of them were wise and five were foolish.

They that were foolish took their lamps and took no oil with them.

But the wise took oil in their vessels with their lamps.

While the Bridegroom tarried they all slumbered and slept.

And at midnight there was a cry, Behold the Bridegroom cometh; go ye out to meet Him.

Then all those virgins rose and trimmed their lamps.

And the foolish said unto the wise, Give us of your oil for our lamps are gone out.

But the wise answered, saying, Not so, lest there be not enough for us and you; but go ye rather to them that sell and buy for yourselves.

And while they went to buy, the Bridegroom came; and they that were ready went in with Him to the marriage; and the door was shut.

I never doubted the Bridegroom would be back. Nor did I doubt that when he returned I should want him to find me among the virgins who were wise. Only I knew from the beginning I should be found among the fools.

I knew this with sadness and certainty. I knew I should be one of the five whose lamps would splutter and die, and would be sent to seek more oil in the hurly-burly of the bazaar while the wise waited in the cool and the calm of the wedding hall.

I knew that I, with the rest, would be caught up in the crush and the colour of the market place, that I should be lost among the silks, the precious stones and the bric-à-brac; that jostling, bargaining, fingering the silver and the gold, I should suddenly realize with horror the passed hours. I knew that I should run, hot and panting, back along the road to the wedding hall, cursing my folly as I ran, and that there I should find the great oak doors closed against me.

Even now I can feel the brass of the lamp in my hand, the fall of the flames beneath my fingers. Even now I can hear the whispers and sighs of the virginhood echoing around the marble.

And there in the last flicker of my lamp I see into my life. And I see I'm not there for the crash of the bolts and the crack of the doors that welcomes the Bridegroom home.

*

The card says Uncle Ezra's been called home. It says he kept the faith and I believe it.

For years I hated Uncle Ezra. He preached the sermon at my mother's funeral, trawling dispassionately for souls among the tears.

The villagers who had turned up to pay their last respects in kindly, country fashion, shrugged off his sermonizing. They dismissed it with the knowing look and the half-shake of the head with which they dismissed all the oddities which over the years marked us out as God-fearing in a village which believed in keeping God in his place.

But Uncle Ezra persisted. He told them of sin and salvation, of the decision that must be made, of the choice of redemption or damnation, a seat at the right hand of the Father or outer darkness with weeping, wailing and gnashing of teeth.

He told them of the wonders and horrors of the Second Coming, of those who would stay when the Last Trumpet sounded and those who would be caught up to heaven in that last, mighty moment.

Uncle Ezra stared out over the coffin. He turned his pleading eyes upon the congregation and, arms open wide begged them, willed them to lay their souls at the foot of the cross, to save themselves.

For Uncle Ezra, seeing their upturned faces, saw them on that last day, their faces upturned still but in despair, watching as the saints ascended above them into glory.

For Uncle Ezra believed in the Second Coming with utter conviction so that if the heavens had opened then and there during his message he would have been gratified, perhaps triumphant, but not a bit surprised.

For Uncle Ezra was one of the Brethren, a man who depended not upon faith for his conviction, but upon a sense of his absolute indispensability to the Almighty.

And so it was that afterwards, at the graveside, he shook my hand sturdily with words of consolation.

Only a little while, Maud, he said, only a little while.

But now Uncle Ezra's been called home. No last mighty moment, just a sleepy, slipping away from life, after the meeting, on a Sunday night, in his old fireside chair, his Bible still open upon his knees.

Imagine a moment between life and death when the ghostly form of the resurrected Ezra steps from the earthly body.

See him look down with affection at the old, eternally

sleeping self. See him lift from the floor the old wire-rimmed glasses which have fallen from the old old hand.

See him place them, gently, upon the table and then see the new Ezra, gone, gone from the room, not to rest but to glory.

See him, not at the front gate of Paradise, but around the side, at some small private door, known only to the few.

See him patting his pocket and finding the key.

See him let himself in, to straighten the chairs and lay out the hymn books. To open up Paradise just as he had opened up the Meeting a hundred thousand times before.

See Uncle Ezra await the Almighty, folding his hands, inclining his head, standing, in fearless self-effacement, before the throne.

*

Matthew and Mikey and Corrie and me. Always the four of us, always the four of us together.

I love Matthew so much that I marry him. I wear an old lace curtain, pinned with May blossoms to my head. I carry primroses picked from the bank of the ditch and periwinkles from the hedge and Corrie is my bridesmaid.

My father, I remember, is enchanted and stops work to rush into the house to get his old Box Brownie before which we pose. The wedding party.

Yes, we are always together. Except for Sundays.

I see Matthew and Mikey and Corrie then scampering outside my window while I'm inside the house, all hushed and Sunday silent.

They stare at me, curious and puzzled, as I come out two, three times a day, in my Sunday best to drive off with my parents. They sit on the railing and they stare, not unfriendly, just puzzled, curious and puzzled.

*

Looking back it seems now as if all those summers were hot and all those winters ice-cold and crackling.

Closing my eyes I think I can still feel the warmth of the huge,

3

hexagonal slabs on the top of the waterfall where we lay, naked, our bodies dappled by sunshine spattering through the canopy of trees that clung to the sides of the little valley. I think I can still feel the ice-cold of the water in the pool beneath and the smell of its heavy, mossy sweetness.

I can see in my mind's eye a blue I never saw again, a fresh, soft, undisturbed blue of early morning, cracked by the sound of a cow lowing far away and mysterious.

Then I can see the four of us, Matthew and Mikey and Corrie and me, one sharp and icy morning, stamping our feet and shuffling with the others around the schoolmistress who is trying to coax the old school stove into life.

I see us singing a hymn to keep warm and the school-mistress turning the pages of her Bible in mittened hands. I see us bent over our arithmetic, shivering, while she paces, angrily, around the cold, silent stove.

And then I see her clapping her hands with a muffled whumpf, forgetting her mittens and saying, Go home, go home, it's too cold to work, so that books are dashed into desks and we run, jumping and whooping out of the door to slide on the icy puddles outside.

I can see myself now in the meeting, sitting where we always sit, three rows from the front in the shadow of the pulpit.

It is a winter's night and the air is thick with warmth from the old brown heating pipes that hiss quietly behind their ugly mesh coverings.

To keep out the cold of the night I wear a fawn, full-skirted little coat with a brown velvet collar. On my head is a small brown hat, a hat that looks as though it is trying to grow up to be just like all the other grown-up hats in the Hall, as I am trying to grow up to be just like the women who wear them.

I am standing now, pretending to sing, lisping foolish and tuneless, swaying and pressing my legs against the seat of the hard, wooden chair.

Ahead of me is the large, dark shape of the organ and behind it my mother, moving back and forwards, side to side,

4

with the rhythm, her rings clicking lightly on the keys, her legs stretching for the floor pedals.

Straining to catch her eye as she reaches for a note, I catch instead the eye of the awkward, short-trousered schoolboy with a thatch of fair hair, who sits on the box at the end of the organ, pumping its handle up and down. He falters for a moment as we stare at each other and the chord dips away breathily before he looks away and begins to pump energetically again.

Disappointed and casting around for more fun, I meet the eyes of the speaker, standing in the pulpit looking down on us like a general, at battle, rallying his troops. He frowns slightly as his eyes meet mine. He continues to sing as we stare at each other before lifting his eyes away to cast them over the bowed heads of the singing congregation.

The hymn finishes and I sit down, wriggling back on my seat. Next to me is Aunt Esther, wife of Uncle Ezra.

He sits away from us on the other side of the Hall at the front. In this spot, now, he alone of us has remained on his feet. He has reached into his pocket for a notebook with a band around it which he has now removed in a movement practised of many Sundays.

Uncle Ezra is reading the notices now, his gold spectacles slipping down his nose a little as he announces the prayer meeting, the women's meeting, the Bible class, the Lord's Supper and the Sunday School, and here again next week, DV, God willing, the Gospel Service.

My mother meanwhile has left her seat behind the organ and has settled down in a chair next to Aunt Esther. To her left is my father who leans forward now, as he always does, to rest his chin on his hand, his arm on his knee, the better to catch the words of the message.

And now the speaker is preaching the word, telling the gospel story, telling it to those who already know it so well, passing on the good news to those who have heard it so many times before.

Sometimes he leans confidingly towards us, sometimes he steps back looking fierce and angry. Sometimes he reads from his Bible, grasping the wooden shelf on which it rests, jabbing it with a stern finger. Sometimes he brandishes it in the air, daring us to disagree with its words.

Everyone listens but me. Instead I scribble loudly and deliberately in a little notebook Aunt Esther always brings for me along with a little brown pencil.

Each Sunday night she brings it and each Sunday I play this game, scribbling like this to attract her attention.

For when I am naughty like this she will do as she is doing now. She will lay her fingers upon mine in the gentlest of restraints and will smile her special smile, that warmest most understanding of smiles that swallows up the year and holds us, this naughty, bored little girl and this woman, in a moment of unholy sympathy.

One day I shall learn that Aunt Esther's heart yearns to worship its maker in surroundings and ceremonies more rich and mysterious than these.

I shall find out that, sometimes, believing herself to be unobserved, Aunt Esther slips into the old village church and there sits, sometimes, for an hour at a time alone.

For one day, spotting her, head down and hurrying up the churchyard path, I shall follow her. Letting myself into the church I shall see her sitting perfectly still in a pew near the back. But the door creaks and Aunt Esther hearing it turns and discovers me.

She beckons me then to her side. Sitting beside her, silently, her arm about me, I see her staring before her at the intricately carved wooden screen and at the decorated altar beyond and then up at the gaudy, glowing stained glass, as if drinking them all in greedily.

I see her then dab her eyes, and following her gaze I find it resting on the figure of the naked, bleeding Christ upon the cross.

Eventually she shakes herself a little and smiles as if at some sad and private joke.

Sauntering to the door as we leave I cast a look over my shoulder and see her standing uncertainly in the aisle before the altar, as if trying to make up her mind about something.

6

Then she drops a faint, hesitant, half-curtsy, turning in a quick movement as if already regretful at what she has done and walks, head down, towards me at the door.

*

We never kneel you see, we the Brethren.

We sing, all the time, At the Name of Jesus Every Knee Shall Bow. But we sing it standing upright, ramrod straight. We sing it smiling quietly to ourselves, knowing it means the knees of others, never our own.

And I never will be able to kneel. Even years on, at weddings, where those unaccustomed to such ceremonies clatter and drop in all the wrong places without embarrassment, still I am unable to do it, easily, with amusement, along with the rest.

One day many years on, I shall have to kneel in a play. An actor will place his hands upon my head in benediction. As he does so I shall feel a thrill, strange, shocking, almost sensuous.

I shall feel that to kneel like this, to feel his hands upon my head, is somehow pagan, even wicked, I shall feel, even after all this time, that to kneel does not belong to what I am.

*

There's a hymn that we sing, a hymn that we know so well that we do not need to look at the hymn books.

When we sing it our faces are raised up and shining. Sometimes we close our eyes when we sing it, or shake our heads slightly in emphasis at its words, or tilt them back, raising our chins, in the glory of it. We sing:

Whiter than the snow
Whiter than the snow
Wash me in the blood of the Lamb
And I shall be whiter than the snow

I cannot read the words yet from the hymn book, but I can sing them. And although I do not understand them, I understand what they mean to me.

I understand them in the way that I understand the words of

7

the painted text that descends the pale blue wall behind the pulpit in a long, thin, golden scroll that looks like a ribbon flung there by a giant hand.

Many times the Sunday School superintendent points at the text and reads it to us slowly and sternly, making us chant it after him. It says, Except a man be born again he cannot enter the Kingdom of Heaven.

I am a child and I know little but I know this one thing. I know I must be born again. I know I must be washed in the blood of the Lamb. I know I must be saved.

How can I know this, just a child in a child's coat and an old woman's hat, a child still learning to write her own name, a child scarcely off the breast.

Because I sucked the gospel with my mother's milk, that's why. How else could it be that I knew my need to be saved before I knew my own name.

I cannot say what sin is but I know that I have sinned.

I cannot say what saved is but I know I must be saved.

I must be saved or else I shall be lost, separated for eternity from those I love, left behind upon the earth while my mother, my father, Aunt Esther and Uncle Ezra ascend above me to glory.

*

Yet in the village school I sit with the rest to hear the vicar give us our weekly religious instruction.

He writes disjointed words and phrases upon the blackboard which we cannot read or understand. Sometimes he forgets the white stick in his hand is chalk so that he puts it to his lips like a cigarette, drawing it back sharply surprised when it touches them.

Once outside the school he stands on the steps and takes immediately from his pocket a packet of Woodbines, one of which he lights up, inhaling it deeply and blowing out the smoke in one long, satisfying breath.

At the end of each class he makes us chant the catechism. It means nothing to me. Why should it? Each morning at school we spend an hour chanting things I do not understand, tables, words difficult to spell, snatches of poetry.

How more strange and remote is the catechism than seven sevens, or Mississippi or verses about someone wandering around like a cloud?

*

One day we're sitting, the four of us, Matthew and Mikey, Corrie and me, on an old piece of pipe we prop up on an oil drum to use as a cannon to fight off invaders.

Big Bessie, though, is at peace now. We sit on her, elbows on knees, chins on our hands. Boredom always threatens like this when the enemy rests.

Becoming restless we sway and push against each other, trying to annoy.

Suddenly Matthew jumps up. He clasps his hands together and closes his eyes.

Then in a voice like the vicar's he begins to pray.

Our Father which art in heaven, he prays. Harold be thy name.

He lets out a big, gurgling laugh then and in case we have missed the joke, says it again, Harold be thy name, Harold be thy name.

His gurgling laugh and the joke begin to ooze out over us. Mikey and Corrie start to giggle and soon they are holding their stomachs and weeping with laughter, laughing at the joke and at Matthew too dancing from foot to foot like a crazy leprechaun, gurgling over and over again, Harold be thy name.

I want to laugh too. I want to laugh like them. But I'm frightened although I'm not sure what of. But just watching them is making my lips curve up and now it is making me chuckle.

I am letting out my first giggle of pleasure when around the corner appears my mother.

To me, sitting on Big Bessie, she looks like one of the avenging angels I had seen in my Bible storybook.

She is carrying a tray of hot ash from the stove to the dustbin and appears to us from behind a cloud of smoke and heat.

She cries, Stop it, Stop it, so that Matthew's Harold be thy name, dies away mid-sentence and he lowers a dancing foot to the ground.

Mikey and Corrie stop laughing too and along with Matthew stare open-mouthed at her while I try to make myself smaller, try to pretend that I am not here, that I have crawled away somehow from her and from her anger.

She dumps the rush of hot coals with a steaming hiss into the ash-can, damp from a fresh shower of rain.

Then she turns to us, Don't ever do that again, she says.

Don't let me ever hear you making jokes about Our Father again, any of you, ever.

She says it slowly and angrily, raking her eyes over the four of us and finishing with one fierce stare at me. And then she is gone.

It is all quiet then, a quiet that seems to go on and on. I become aware that the other three are looking at me, quizzically, surreptitiously, from beneath lowered eyes, as if there was something new and different about me, as if I had suddenly become an object of curiosity.

Then Matthew, still standing in the spot where he had danced, begins to shake his copper-coloured head, slowly from side to side, as if in confusion.

He begins to whistle softly through his teeth as if pondering carefully his next move. Then he turns and scuffs slowly and nonchalantly over to his bike which is lying nearby on the ground.

Then he is up and on it and off, standing high on the saddle and whistling softly, pedalling slowly and easily around the corner.

Mikey and Corrie get up then like puppets, pulled to life by the same unseen hand. They stroll away together without looking back, snapping blue periwinkles from the hedge as they go.

And then I am left alone on Big Bessie, alone and unmoving, alone with the vaporous cloud of ash falling and settling and covering everything it touches with a dull, miserable film.

*

Only a little while, Maud, they say, only a little while.

And that's how we live our lives, waiting always waiting. All so

10

many souls, looking upwards and ahead, waiting for the clouds to roll back, listening for the sound of the trumpets, watching for the seven gold candlesticks, waiting, waiting, waiting for the seal to be broken and the book to be opened and He Who Only Is Worthy to call us by name.

Watch and pray, Maud, they say, watch and pray.

We're in the last days now, Maud. See the wickedness, Maud, the ungodliness. The time is at hand now, Maud, the time of the bottomless pit, of the lake of fire, the time for men to run to the hills and to call on the rocks, Rocks cover us.

But not for us, Maud, not for us. We shall be all in white, Maud, around the throne, Maud, reflected in the sea of glass. We shall see the river of life, Maud, clear as crystal, and the Tree of Life, Maud.

There will be no night there, Maud, they say, there will be no night, or hunger, Maud, or thirst. Or weeping. God will wipe all tears from our eyes, Maud, they say.

And till then we wait, Maud, wait for the better place, in this world not our home, wait for the new heaven and the new earth, wait on the old earth for the day that it passes away.

Only a little while, Maud, they say, only a little while.

*

Faithfully each Sunday comes a plump and soft-faced widow to the Hall.

Her head is always slightly bent, her eyes always, just a little, cast down. She eases herself into her seat, respectful and deferential, shooting low darting smiles of acknowledgement to those around her.

Humility is required of all of us, Brethren women, our lives passed, hand to hand, from God to our fathers and to our husbands.

But a special humility is required of her because she sinned and would not seek repentance, because she, Brethren woman, married a farmer, middle-aged, merry and non-believing, and lived with him in happiness for twenty years.

He thought more of his pint and his pipe than he did of her

God but he bent to her will on Sunday nights and when she came home from the meeting played her hymns on his concertina instead of the music hall songs he loved so much better.

Faithfully during twenty years of marriage she stuck firmly to her faith, he to his disregard. When he died, crushed into the soil by his ancient tractor on a lonely hillside, she sought no extra spiritual consolation nor yet lost her faith.

She just came, morning and night, as before, quiet and respectful. Until one night, not long before she dies, when she comes for the last time.

That night I see her, staring down at her Bible, long after the last prayer has been said and people have moved from their seats and are gossiping on their way to the door.

But she just sits and when I move alongside her I see that her Bible is open at the story of the healing of the woman with the issue of blood, the woman who is cured by touching the hem of Jesus' garment.

It is the passage on which the speaker has been preaching and as I sit down beside her I see her finger is still moving slowly along the lines and her lips mouthing wordlessly.

And then she speaks, without raising her head, as if talking to no one but merely musing out loud.

Thirty years I've been coming here, she says. Thirty years and still I creep in.

I'm just like her, stealing in, stealing in just to touch the hem of His garment.

I hear her voice still, full of old repressed anger and pain but full too of determination and self-discovery. I see myself looking at her, young, curious and uncomprehending.

It is the last time she comes to the hall.

She does not answer the door when they come to enquire for her. They say when they knock they hear odd sounds like the sound of a concertina badly played.

Behind their hands they say she has grown old and a little soft in the head.

I think no more about her that night and scarcely think of her

12

again until many years on when I am paying a sad and awkward visit to Uncle Ezra.

Waiting for him in his study I turn, idly, the pages of a large leatherbound volume on his desk which I know to be a record of the meetings of the elders going back many years.

Suddenly her name leaps out at me from the prices of cleaning powder and communion wine and what I read affects me with such violence that I slump down upon the old carved chair by the desk.

Uncle Ezra's hand, cold, precise and clerical tells me she has been seen going into a little shop around the corner from the Hall, one Sunday morning before the meeting and has been seen, further, to emerge with a small packet of tobacco for the merry farmer, which she then has slipped into her handbag.

The neat, inexorable hand tells me that after discussion it is decided that an elder shall have a quiet word with her about this breaking of the Sabbath, this shopping for, of all things, tobacco on a Sunday.

I close my eyes, then, even now, to try and cut out the horror of that quiet word.

I see her leaving the Hall the next Sunday, her meek, forever slightly bent head the eternal acknowledgement of her ongoing imperfection.

I see her extend her hand at the door for the handshake of farewell and blessing, only this time I see her hand held a little longer and I see her drawn aside by the elder to a corner of the Hall.

I see his head inclining and fatherly as he speaks, hers still and bowed. I feel with her the stabs of pain as the words pierce her like arrows.

I feel the anger rise inside her like a sickness. I feel her gulp and force it down. And then I see her nod briefly and then summon up a half-smile for this, another's vigilant, selfless concern for her soul, this concern hiding within its kindly exterior an implacable remorselessness which does violence to the spirit. I see him now grasping her limp sad hand, forgiving

13

and magnanimous. I see her walking home alone in sadness and anger, in tears of shame and pain.

Oh yes, we had our plaster saints you see, we the Brethren. We made our graven images. And it seems to me significant now that we set upon the pedestal not the Virgin, the glorious, shameless mother of Christ, but the woman who stole to his side, the woman who touched his hem, the woman who was healed and restored, made whole and rewarded for a proper show of respect, for a proper show of humility.

*

The baptism pit lies in the corner of the Hall. I always know it is there. It never frightens me until one day I see it open, gaping at me, the floorboards that normally keep it hidden standing out of place against the wall.

After this its presence persecutes me, even after it is covered up again.

I seem to feel the pit beneath my feet when I walk over it. I leave the collection of the hymn books there to others, thinking, maybe in my sinful state the floorboards will collapse and hurl me down to the pit beneath. For I am not saved yet, not yet ready to pass through the waters of baptism.

Water for the baptism pit is run in from two little brass taps at one end. It is waist high and glitters, incongruous and dangerous in the place where the floor should be, its warmth making the atmosphere at the baptism heavy, humid and doubly solemn.

Most often Uncle Ezra does the baptism. The water flattens his trousers against his legs and with his shirt sleeves rolled up he looks just like one of the farmers in the village waiting in the sheep dip for the next animal. Seeing a farmer like this I still think, unfailingly, of Uncle Ezra.

No farmer baptizes his sheep, either, with a quicker, neater movement.

There's the vow of belief and then a deep, long splash which seems to reverberate around the Hall as Uncle Ezra's wiry shop-keeper's arms plunge the candidate back, bringing them up again, man or woman, controlled and easy.

14

They stand then, confused and trying to regain their balance, water streaming from hair and eyes. And then they struggle to the side of the pool where outstretched arms stretch to help them.

Then, sodden and weeping a little, they hurry through the singing congregation looking for all the world like survivors from some disaster caught by the newsreel.

As they pass me I turn away in fear and embarrassment. I shiver in the warm air at the sight of the water-bruised face, at the sight of the wringing hair and tears.

I screw my eyes tight shut as they pass in a violent rush of disgust and horror. I bury my face with my fear in my hymn book and I say to myself, Only a little while, Maud, only a little while.

*

Uncle Ezra was converted in the trenches in the First World War, a freckle-faced soldier of eighteen.

Standing sentry in a company of putrifying corpses, exploding shells punctuating the moans from no-man's land, Uncle Ezra perceived himself to be in hell and thus was filled with a desire to be sure of heaven.

And then my mother, suffering from TB and locked away in a drab, unfriendly sanatorium in the hills, fevered and frightened one night, called out into the dark, Jesus Save Me.

Which makes me feel hard done by, child that I am and sets me wondering how I can be saved without a war or a disease to bring it about.

*

For there has to be a moment. All my life it is preached to me, prayed to me. That there must be this occasion, when seeing suddenly my sin, I shall know my need to repent. I shall see my need to be saved and shall do as Uncle Ezra did, bowing his head momentarily upon his rifle, as my mother did, crying in desperation out into the night.

Once, only once, Matthew comes to our Sunday School. My

15

mother persuades his parents to send him and so he sits, awkward and angry and deprived of his liberty, in his boy's best suit, in the back of our car as we drive to the Hall.

The Sunday School superintendent, a large man, fleshy and stern, being unhappy in the presence of children becomes oily and wheedling in his efforts to teach and convert us.

He has a routine he performs like Buttons in a pantomime and he does it the day Matthew comes.

Leaning confidentally towards us from the pulpit, as if not sure of the reply he has heard a hundred times before, he asks us, Do you like birthdays, children?

Knowing our part well, we answer, Yes.

Would you like two? he asks.

We chorus Yes again.

I am gawping and chorusing along with the rest when I catch sight of Matthew. He is staring open-mouthed at the Superintendent, his feet dangling, not quite touching the ground, shocked and still. There is a look of horror upon his face.

As the Superintendent goes on to tell us how we should be Born Again and earn ourselves our Second Birthday, Matthew's look of horror changes to one of scorn, a scorn so searing it makes him look old, more like a dwarf than a little boy.

Afterwards he sits hunched in a corner of the car refusing to speak, refusing even to meet my eye. He never comes again to our Sunday School does Matthew.

It is about this time that I begin to dream this dream. I dream I'm hiding in the corner of a huge, dusty old room filled with trunks and boxes, covered in cobwebs.

Into the room come men in dark suits, holding Bibles that shine like torches. Their beams sweep around the room, over the cobwebbed mildewed jumble. Cowering in the corner I close my eyes tight shut in terror, I draw up my legs, straining my coat over me, trying in agony to cover the dreadful thing that I hide.

But then I feel their light upon my face. Opening my eyes I see their dark shapes behind the brightness of their beams. I bend my head in despair for I know they have found me and the dirty

16

sin-covered soul that I am hugging lovingly to myself as I huddle in the corner.

I am frightened now of the farewell handshakes at the door of the hall. I think of the elders as the men in my dream.

Dark suited and serious, they shake my hand as I leave and I think as they look deep into my eyes that they see down into my soul.

I think I can feel a disturbing pressure in their grip, a questioning in their fingers that is echoed in their eyes, that makes their simple God Bless You not a blessing at all, but an interrogation, a demand. A demand whether all be right with my soul.

*

I am eleven when I first give my testimony. I have been working up to it for some time. I think that if I say I am saved, publicly, the questioning in the fingers will stop. I tell myself it may be true, I may be saved. That not having a war, or a dark, sick night to call out into, I may have missed the moment.

So here I am at last, standing by the wheezing old pedal organ at home, watching my mother dusting beneath the hymn books and the sacred music piled on the top, waiting to tell her the good news.

For several days I have tried to catch her alone like this. But now I have the opportunity it seems the words will not come. I know what I must say but suddenly I cannot say it.

Something physical is holding me back. I am clearing my throat, drawing back my lips, trying to force out the words. But they will not come.

My jaw is rigid, my teeth clamped, tightly shut, guarded by my lips as if, all together, they object to what I am about to say and will do their best to prevent me saying it.

I overpower them though and as I do so the words hurl forward and out into the air.

I want to be baptized, I say. I've taken Jesus as my own personal saviour.

I say it in a rush, gabbling the words. As if at some huge effort, tears start from my eyes so that I blink to stop them.

I start again, but the words seem to trail away. I'm saved, I say. I'm born again.

The words, all the words, ugly and monstrous hang in the silence.

My mother says nothing, just continues to dust, practised and methodical, rubbing, lifting and stacking the books.

Then she slows down her dusting and stops with a final flick. She looks at me hard and says, You're too young to be baptized.

Then, as if relenting, she smiles and stepping towards me, gives me an odd, awkward, tender hug.

And then she says, formally, again, I'm pleased you told me. Now you must tell Uncle Ezra.

And then she is gone and I slump down on the organ stool, weak with relief and weak also from a strange new feeling of sickness that is physical and yet compounded of shame and embarrassment and seems to reach down somewhere deep inside me.

I roll the words that I have said over in my mind. I grind the words like 'personal saviour' into my brain. I force myself to repeat their awful intimacy and as I do so their horror seems to overwhelm me so that I lay my head, heavy with their weight, upon the music stand. As I do so the tears that had started but were held back begin again and continue, unabated, on their course.

*

When I become a woman, I shall nurse all this with loving care. I shall bleed it, you might say. I shall come to think of it as quite my best feature. I shall wear it, like a brooch, upon my shoulder, slip it on with my shoes, pin it up in my hair.

When I am lonely I shall cling to it, for consolation, use it to hide my inadequacies at parties, use it to warm me in the chill of misplaced early mornings.

Best of all, though, I shall like to pour it into the eyes and ears of lovers, my pain a love potion, old strictures, shamelessly employed to guarantee the new.

I shall tell them, kind, indistinct young men, tales of an

embittered adolescence so that they will love me. And sometimes they will and, seeking to help me to exorcise my demons, will press me to tell them more.

But what exactly do the Brethren believe? they will ask.

And I shall be unable to answer. For as I try to speak it will seem to me that the words lodge inside me. I shall feel them caught, as of old, in the tightening of my throat, straining as of old against my jaw and teeth and lips.

There comes a day though when I don't tell tales any more, when I have no use for love potions and think that all that happened to have happened in the past and being so, to be long since dead and gone.

And so, it comes as a surprise when asked the old, familiar question, to feel again the long forgotten tightening of the throat, the firmness of the jaw, the clamping of the teeth.

It comes as a surprise to find them all still banding themselves together in this way, still throwing up their old defences against my words' betrayal.

*

I can see myself now, in the Hall again. It is a Sunday morning. I wear my Sunday best, my white frilled blouse with a suit of pale mauve check and a smart white straw hat that is already a little too dashing to ever be quite like the other hats in the Hall.

Before me the April sun streams through the high mock-Gothic windows dancing its rays on the white cloth of the communion table, on the silver plate with its cottage loaf and on the silver cup and the goblet of wine.

This is the Morning Meeting, the Lord's Supper, the Breaking of the Bread, a time of devotion and fellowship when we sing hymns of Christian service, mournful and unaccompanied.

Between them we sit silent, waiting for the spirit to move among us, to light upon the shoulder of a Brother, directing him to speak or to pray.

Waiting, eyes closed between the hymns, I am shocked to

hear the scrape of a chair close to my own. I open my eyes to see my father on his feet for the first time in the Morning Meeting in my memory.

Then I close them again in embarrassment hearing him struggle earnestly, Bible in hand, grappling among the words, limping and stuttering, trying desperately to explain the thought that has grasped at his heart.

As his words hiccup and meander, I begin to blush hot with shame. I stare into my Bible at the text he has chosen. The words blur before my eyes and as they do I begin to pray. I screw my eyes tight shut and I pray fervently. I pray, Dear God, please make him stop and sit down.

*

I never do tell Uncle Ezra about being saved. I feel good for a while though, after my testimony. I even think I am saved so I set the alarm early to read my Bible and pray before school. And it feels good. But it doesn't last.

Things are beginning to change, anyway. My body, for instance, is moving slowly, mysteriously from child to woman, with my mind skipping along beside it, sometimes behind, sometimes in front.

I want new things. Most of all I want to be just like everyone else, just like the rest of the girls at the grammar school where I have gone from the little village schoolroom.

For the grammar school is inhospitable to oddness. There is no tide of village life to close over our eccentricity here and strange new girlish rites of passage are driving a wedge through the sameness I felt once with Matthew, Mikey and Corrie.

Like the dirty joke I do not understand. I know only one fact of life. You fall in love and get married and God makes everything right. Like the ballroom dancing class I cannot go to along with the rest. My mother tells me, as I recall, You can't serve Jesus on the dance floor. Like the young and zealous curate who tries to canvass me along with the rest for confirmation. He shakes his head at me, pityingly, when he sees me in the corridor after my mother writes a letter telling him to stop.

20

For my mother reserves her greatest scorn for confirmation. A matter not of faith, she calls it, but frocks. And she should know for as village dressmaker she does a steady trade in confirmation dresses.

She crawls upon the floor, tucking and pulling, taking pins from lips clamped tight with displeasure as the child turns and twists before the mirror and the fond mama oohs and aahs with joy.

Later, she bends over the machine, a strange, unhappy genius, adrift in a sea of silk and tulle and lace, stitching and fastening together beautiful creations she has no wish to call her own.

It is the same when she makes a gown for my first ball of which she totally disapproves.

It is a dress of such loveliness that I keep it for years, long after it is out of fashion.

While the other girls gambol, pretty, pastel creatures in bell skirts with necklines scooped gently to show peeping, milk-white breasts, I stand, straight as a boy, in a column of severe and unrelenting black.

She hates the dress as she sews its disturbing beauty. She looks away as I admire myself in the mirror, as I place my hands upon its straightness and turn slowly. Instead she stares fixedly at the material, sticking the pins coldly around the body which her every gesture refuses to acknowledge as mine.

It is the last dress she sews before she dies. I go to the ball in it with Frank. He says, You look beautiful, and turning to look at myself in the mirrored ballroom wall as we pass, I think he is probably right.

2

I give my testimony for the second time at a Christian youth camp where I have gone with some girls from my school. I am having such fun, learning from them to peer around and make faces during prayers, learning to smirk and to nudge during the Bible reading. Which makes it all the more surprising that I do what I do.

It is the last night of the camp. We are sitting, the thirty or so of us girls, around a huge bonfire which crackles and blazes, throwing showers of sparks up into the warm, late summer night.

The heat reddens our faces and lights them up against the dark of the night behind us as we sit cross-legged, singing old choruses of faith. We have linked arms, and are turning and smiling at each other, rocking and swaying from side to side with the songs. We have been together for only a week and yet we feel like sisters, warmed inside and out by the fire and the night and the clear sweet unity of the female voice.

Leaping from song to song, the singing eventually dies away and one of the leaders asks if there is anyone who wishes to say what the camp has meant to her.

Behind the flames I see the girls from my school exchange glances, mocking and adult and knowing.

A girl sitting near me rises hesitantly to her feet and begins to speak, haltingly, of friendship and love, and then finally of Jesus.

She sits down, bowing her head as she does as if acknowledging some silent sentence. Another rises almost immediately as if her part is next and begins talking of a change, of a new life. There are others then, two more, scrambling to their feet, one close upon the other. Until there is silence, sudden and overwhelming.

Perhaps it is this silence that does it. I think so, yes, the silence, like the silence at the Morning Meeting that hangs upon the air after a hymn or a prayer, that seems alive and rings in your ears and thumps at your heart and calls for a voice.

Yes, I think it is the silence that pushes me to my feet so that I see too late the sight of the girls whom I want to be so much like, looking at me curiously through the flames.

On my feet, my face lit up a fiery red by the fire and a rising flush of embarrassment, I hesitate but then burst furiously into life.

I begin to babble, words, nonsensical words, words used by the girls who had risen before me, old words, words of the preachers, words I said once before to my mother but dared not say to Uncle Ezra.

It seems to me as I hear the words streaming out into the night that I am trying to stop up the silence. But it is impossible for even as I rush on I seem to feel it hanging all about, mocking the demented rush of sound that I recognize with horror as my own voice.

At the sound of such foolishness I become suddenly sick with fear and with fear comes desperation. As the words pour on I begin to fling my arms around, raising and dropping them, begging and imploring, in horrible parody of the preacher.

And so the words hurtle out, spewing from an old store somewhere inside me. I hear them as they pass my lips but am powerless to stop them.

Eventually when it seems to me that I have been on my feet hours, gabbling and gesticulating, I sit down, suddenly, surprising both myself and the others.

And now there is silence but this time a real silence, shocked and deeply satisfied, a silence filled up and satiated and complete in itself.

Back on the ground I feel weak with shame but, at the same time, oddly elated.

A log falls from the fire shooting up flames and sparks into the air, shaking us all into life. The sudden shaft of light falls upon the bright unblinking curiosity of the girls from my school who are staring at me now, open-mouthed and still, through the rising and falling of the flames.

Later as the group breaks up to go to bed, I wait by the side of the fire till they have gone to the tent. I am last to the wooden wash-houses, dragging out my teeth cleaning till the last girl has left.

Only then I walk back to the tent. Inside the old lamp has already been turned out. I undress in the darkness and drag myself drained and despairing into my sleeping bag.

And then I hear another new silence, a silence alive and aloud with the sound of stifled, girlish giggles, a silence trembling on the edge of open laughter.

I turn my face to my pillow then and close my eyes. Before me rises up the image of myself, red-faced and gesticulating before the fire. I hear the babble of sound again in my ears. And there in the blackness I bury my head in the pillow to weep silent, bitter tears of anger and absolute self-loathing.

*

Several days later I return to school for the start of the autumn term. I am two days late. I am supposed to have been ill but in truth I have not been unwell at all. I feigned sickness, making myself vomit, to put off the dreadful moment of facing my classmates.

For the morning after the night of my testimony I stayed huddled in my sleeping bag, my head covered till they left the tent. I packed my things quickly while they were at breakfast and ran to the gateway to catch my parents as they arrived in the old Morris Eight. I threw myself at them as they drew up, saying how much I had missed them. They were happy, I remember, and drove home along an especially pretty route, taking me to lunch in a café on the way.

Now though I am slipping, nervous and frightened, into the classroom at five minutes to nine.

I had hoped desperately to be lost in the swell of arrivals but I am unlucky for somehow this morning everyone is here, chattering and laughing as I enter.

24

I slide into a vacant chair but near me a voice says firmly, Taken.

I look up into a pair of eyes that glitter with the delight of some fun to come. They direct me, these eyes, in one swivelling movement to another desk at the very front of the class.

I pick myself up and walk to it slowly and mutely. The room, I realize, has gone silent. I sit down, my whole body feeling heavy and begin to peel off my blazer with arms that feel weighed down with chains.

My right hand catches in a sleeve of the coat and slowly still, as if preoccupied with the action, I tug gently and deliberately to free it. But I fool no one, and as it comes loose and I hang it on the back of my chair I know that everyone is watching me and that they know that I know.

I reach down now and take my pencil case from my satchel. I am like someone performing a ritual and I cannot help but know that a sacrifice is in the air. Everyone is waiting and I recognize again the sound that masquerades as silence but is really a jangle of derision and merriment.

Slowly, very slowly, I raise the lid of the wooden desk. As its carved, marked top, with scribbled names and old sums and phrases rises slowly past my eyes there appears on its underside a gaudy, grinning piece of paper.

It is a text, ribbon-shaped like the one on the Meeting wall, but golden with cherubs and trumpets. It tells me Jesus Saves.

There is an explosion of sound in my ears so that I close my eyes with the sound of it trying to blot out the noise and the sight of the text leering up at me from the desk top.

The explosion is the sound of laughter which is rising from all corners of the classroom and is being swelled by the dull clanging of the bell for assembly.

Laughing and looking at me, the class is moving towards the door. My eyes are open now, open as if they will never close, fixed upon the text as if for always, as if they will never be drawn away.

The classroom is quiet but on and on inside my head the

explosion of their laughter rumbles on. It thunders over and over in great rolls, rising and falling.

But then there is another sound, a sound that makes no sense but which echoes insistently through the rumble until I finally identify it as the sound of my own name.

I look up and see before me the black-gowned shape of a teacher, staring down at me from over the desk top.

Maud, she is saying, what are you doing? What is the matter?

I look at her vacantly for a moment. Then I slam the desk top closed guiltily and jump to my feet.

She continues to stare hard at me as I walk slowly and lifelessly to the door and into the assembly hall.

I squeeze on to the end of a line of girls fumbling with their hymn books and taking their first breaths for a hymn.

I pull the book of the girl next to me towards me but try as I may to sing I keep losing my place on the page. The words keep blurring and receding from my sight, leaving in their place golden cherubs and the Jesus Saves which is still echoing around my brain along with the thunder of laughter.

The cotton dress beneath my armpits is wet and there is a tight feeling of panic in my chest. I feel sick with a new sickness, a real sickness that is creeping down through my body and poisoning it all the way through to its very heart and soul.

Sitting hunched on the floor and listening to the headmistress read a lesson I see suddenly stretched before me Eternity, a life sentence of mocking and sniggering, three more years at this school to be forever odd, forever different.

Sweating and panicky and sick I begin to make foolish childish plans. I'll run away, get a job, sell myself into slavery, anything but face that classroom with its thunder of laughter, its mocking eyes and its wicked, grinning text.

*

Hanging over my bed is a small picture. It will stay with me for many years, refusing to be mislaid or lost, refusing to be broken or given away, refusing to be put out for jumble sales or charity shops.

26

Many times I will think it is gone and will be relieved, even pleased, but then it will turn up again in a box or in the corner of a drawer, unravelling a string of memories, persistent in its pastel sweetness.

All my life the picture will both fascinate and repulse me. It will fill me with a dreadful yearning and also with a rich disgust. I shall look at it with love and with absolute loathing.

Each night as I climb into bed the eyes of the stooping blue-robed stranger will hold mine for a moment, gentle, reproachful pools beneath the dark, ignominious thorns.

Each night, caught in the light of his upraised lantern, the lips will part again in the long low whisper of my name.

And each night, as I look, the loving hand will clench once more to strike at the heavy closed door they tell me is the door of my heart.

*

I do not run away of course. Instead I go back to the classroom and take my seat at my desk, feeling, as I lay my arms along its top, the leer of the text underneath.

I watch the lips of the teacher and hear her voice, so that I turn the pages of the books as she directs. I even answer once when she asks me a question and read a passage out loud. But it seems to me that I see nothing, hear nothing and speak nothing.

I cannot run away because it is only in books that people run away so instead I do all that I can to make myself invisible. I almost believe I have succeeded, so that it comes as a surprise in the cloakroom to see my own face staring back at me above the wash-basin, as it is a surprise, too, to hear a voice reading out loud that I know to be mine.

It seems to me that, if I try hard enough, I can slide slyly out of people's sight and with this in mind I slink along the corridors and strain against the walls. Seeing myself once in a shop window as I pass I see a figure hunched and scurrying, like an animal running from the light.

In the classroom, I hide behind the desk top. The text is gone now. I stayed behind that first day and tore it off. I hesitated before I did it, a little nervous at what I was about to do, but then I ripped it free from the wood in one angry movement, tearing it again and again in tiny pieces and throwing them into the bin.

I turned away quickly as they fluttered in so that none of the pieces should stare back at me accusingly. When I lifted the desk top the following morning I believe I half-expected to see the text there again, half-expected the fluttering scraps of paper to have gathered themselves together during the night and returned themselves to the spot from which they had been torn.

Trying to stay away from those who had witnessed my humiliation, I miss lunch and the sessions at the tuck shop. Sometimes at the end of the day, cycling away from the school grounds, I realize I have not spoken to another person, answered my name in class perhaps, or read out loud, yelled out in hockey, but not spoken, one person to another.

Without the lunches and the tuck shop sweets I become thin and a little pale looking. I seem to be looking constantly over my shoulder, convinced as I am that I am the reason for every glance, or look or overheard remark, the cause of every huddle. I believe myself firmly to be marked out for ever at the school, my class's eternal oddity.

I have a calendar on my bedroom wall on which I mark off the days till the end of term. The first morning of the Christmas holidays I wake with a feeling of relief so strong that I stretch my toes out to the bottom of the bed with the sheer physical pleasure of it, marvelling at the miracle of time which, crawling from hour to hour, has managed to become a whole passed term.

I jump out of bed and dress and, without breakfast, run to the village shop to help Aunt Esther make up and deliver the Saturday orders. It is one of my treats to help her, to stand before the boxes with the blue order books, to take the jars and the tins and packets from the shelves and to pack them neatly and tightly in and then to deliver them around the village.

This morning the crisp, metallic whirr of the slicing machine cutting the ham sounds like a gentle tune and the cheese smiles up at me, yellow and bright, as I draw the wire sharply down through it.

Together Aunt Esther and I pile the boxes into the back of the old green van and stack up the little racks at the side with the extras, the salt and the pepper, the sugar and the tea and the odd pound of round farmhouse butter.

I close the two back doors with their oval windows firmly, turning the handle and then we are off.

Aunt Esther has been driving the old van for as long as I can remember yet today, as always, as I jump into the front seat chattering she says, Not now, dear, not when I'm driving.

And so we drive off together in silence me hugging my knees together and looking about me, Aunt Esther leaning forward tensely, peering fixedly ahead and pushing the long, black-knobbed gearstick forward and back in sharp, jabbing movements.

We trundle along in second, occasionally third gear, on the road which climbs gently at first but then steeply away, out of the village. Around us high clay banks, thick with ferns and spindly trees, clinging to the ground with grasping roots almost shut out the sky.

Today the trees and ferns drip from days of the soft remorseless rain that falls like a curtain on our village. Deep gullies of water wash down on either side of the lane as Aunt Esther guides the van along on the muddy tarmac between them.

We pull up outside farmhouses and cottages, sometimes standing alone, sometimes nestling in twos and threes, parking in yards heavy with the smell of dung and the rich oppressive sweetness of the dairy.

Everywhere we are invited for tea, but Aunt Esther says no until we stop outside a long, low farmhouse, its heavy thatched roof squatting on walls bulging and misshapen and seeming to pop out its tiny windows like eyes.

Getting out of the van, we can see the village below us, cloaked in the misty rain. I can see the shop and the church, the village hall and the pub and my house and a black, ant-like creature which is my father working outside.

29

We nudge open the heavy front door, carrying our boxes and walk along a narrow, stone-flagged corridor with a ceiling so low, its dark beams almost touch our heads.

Aunt Esther makes a soft calling noise, light and feminine and as she does so the latch on a door before us lifts and the door is opened and the farmer's wife is before us.

We pass through with our boxes and drop them on a long, wooden table, scrubbed almost white over many years. At the end of the room is a black range with a kettle steaming upon it. Now there is tea and talk too, idle and warm as the farmer's wife, plump and puffing, eases herself into a chair and Aunt Esther drops nimbly down opposite her. They lean upon the table on their elbows, bending over their cups, their two grey heads nodding gently towards each other.

Their country voices are low and unhurried. They slide their words together and finish each other's sentences as if together weaving a pattern of sound. They are absorbed in their own conversation so that when a farm labourer sticks his head suddenly around the kitchen door to ask a question of the farmer's wife she turns upon him impatiently and sharply and he pulls his head back quickly and closes the door.

Sitting, sipping my tea, I muse as always upon the mysterious circle of dark wood lying beneath the kitchen table, in the stone-flagged floor.

It is the cover to the mouth of a tunnel which they say winds three miles underground, down the hill and beneath the moors to the graceful skeleton of stone which was once the great abbey.

Once a year there is a pilgrimage to the abbey ruins. As the pilgrims pass we close the Hall doors. We close our doors on their priests in their purple cassocks and their bright white shawls, on their incense swinging in delicate, silver burners and on the sound of their chanting.

We close our doors on them and pray for them and we joke that God answers prayers when it rains on Pilgrimage Day.

But I love the abbey. Aunt Esther takes me first when I am very young. We sit in a niche together, she quietly resting her head against the pale yellowy stone. After that I go often with Corrie, on Saturdays, or during the long, lazy days of summer when the abbey is full of visitors. We cycle there taking with us lemonade and sandwiches and picnic beneath the graceful, towering ribs of stone which pierce the sky like fingers, pointing directly to Heaven.

*

Aunt Esther has a way of holding parts of her life to herself, a way of keeping them private with a cool, implacable resistance which will not brook discussion.

So it is that she is able to sit, peaceful and undisturbed in the church or in the abbey and is able also, once a year, to take her place behind the tea urn at that most wicked and worldly of get-togethers, the annual parish party.

This year Aunt Esther, seeing me a little pale and miserable-looking, decides that I shall go with her to the party. When Aunt Esther tells me she will take me and that she will ask my mother, I leap out of my chair with excitement.

For years I have wanted to go to the parish party and I know my mother will say yes. She will say yes, hesitating, unhappy and embarrassed that Aunt Esther has asked but still she will say yes for I think she is a little afraid of Aunt Esther.

I think she is afraid of Aunt Esther because of the way Aunt Esther has of keeping these private places in her life. It makes her uneasy as if something about Aunt Esther is undermining her own way of looking at things. It makes her nervous as if she believes that this something in Aunt Esther is capable of subtly eating away at the foundations of all that is important to her while she stands by, helpless and unable to prevent it.

It bemuses her that Aunt Esther can somehow span the two worlds of the village and the Hall, that some force, hidden from herself, allows Aunt Esther to live this way, holding on to a little of the world so firmly, while keeping a grip, too, on the Kingdom of Heaven.

I don't know. Maybe my mother feels cheated a little. But what hurts most I think is that sometimes she has the feeling that Aunt Esther is laughing at her, not unkindly, but laughing none the less.

Aunt Esther likes a glass of sherry and raises it with a twinkle in her eye and says, For what we are about to receive, which hurts my mother for it is her favourite grace and somehow it seems not quite right, Aunt Esther using it like this.

Also Aunt Esther often calls the Hall 'the kirk' and says, Off to the kirk, then, with her lips twitching and what sounds like a chuckle in her voice as we put on our hats and pick up our Bibles on a Sunday morning.

My mother dare not voice her thoughts, but sometimes she thinks to herself that something mocks at her beneath the chuckle.

And so it is that my mother says yes to Aunt Esther, looking away as she tells me I may go to the parish party, so she will not see my look of disloyal pleasure and will not feel the strange new pang in her heart that if she examined she would find was jealousy.

*

There is a condition, of course, I must be home by ten o'clock. But this does not seem unfair for ten o'clock to me seems wonderfully late. Indeed I cannot imagine delights so wonderful they can only happen beyond this bewitching hour.

I wear a new dress of dark blue, full skirted, with a little black bow at the collar. When I turn before the mirror, the skirt swirls out to show off the stiff white net petticoats underneath. I wear nylon stockings for the first time, hitched up on a wide pink cummerbund of a suspender belt, and a pair of new, black shiny shoes with a tiny heel that makes me feel light and tall and grown up.

I wash my hair and curl it up on pink, plastic rollers so that when it is dry it is a mass of kinks and curls which I brush into a smooth bob. I powder my nose with a little tin compact of powder that I have bought secretly from a chemist, looking all the time over my shoulder as I went in, in case someone should see me, and I put Vaseline on my lips and my eyelids to make them shine.

Walking in through the doors the hall looks to me the most beautiful, the most exciting place I have ever seen. Of course I have been here before, but just for jumble sales, not when it was dressed up like this with gaudy streamers and Chinese lanterns and dark clumps of holly and mistletoe.

It is filled, too, with the prettiest sound I have ever heard, a polka played by three musicians sitting upon the stage.

I find Aunt Esther in the kitchen, her face bright with pleasure and heat behind the silver urn. Together we heave huge tin jugs of water from the white china sink to pour into the urn. Then we set the cups out on long trestle tables in a side room. I do my part quickly, dropping spoons several times for I am anxious to be back in the magical place next door.

Soon the tables are surrounded with women carrying huge trays of food and Aunt Esther is lost among their chattering crush so that I am able to slip away and back into the hall.

The band is playing a quickstep now and several couples are dancing around the floor. They glide sedately as if in a dream, couples who have danced half a life together, some of them, holding up their arms like puppets.

Around the room stand knots of people watching and chattering, nodding at new arrivals and calling hellos. Others sit in groups at tables set with dazzling white cloths which stand around the edge of the room. Children race up and down the sidelines while the adults dance, swooping in and out of the tables and causing the women who are still entering with their trays of sandwiches, jellies and home-made cakes, to weave and bend to safety.

I see Corrie lounging against a wall and move to join her. Together we watch the local policeman in an old and dusty evening suit play Master of Ceremonies, laughing at him a little.

Then I am aware of a sidling presence next to us. It is Matthew and Mikey, but a changed Matthew and Mikey, two grown-up young men in tailor's window suits, white shirts an thin ties, slicked back hair and shining, pointed shoes.

To my surprise Mikey leads Corrie away for a lemonade, no

longer trotting behind her as he used to do but walking with her and once even laying his hand upon her arm to steer her through the milling people.

For some reason what I see makes me feel strange with Matthew and I lounge against the wall trying to feel the old ease and unconcern of childhood.

People are dribbling into the centre of the hall now, forming themselves into a line for a game.

Daft this, says Matthew. I nod, importantly, as if I agree but even the silly game seems wonderful to me.

Surprised to see you here, says Matthew.

Aunt Esther, I say, I'm with Aunt Esther.

Matthew nods as a whistle blows. The band begins to play a gallop as people run up and down tossing bean-bags.

Aunt Esther's friend, the fat farmer's wife wobbling with weight and good humour, lands with a hollow smack upon the floor as she reaches to catch a bean-bag.

Matthew hoots, hands in pockets, bending his legs in his thin, tight trousers and sticking out his elbows. I try not to laugh, turning my head away as the woman gets up, unhurt and unworried. As she does so there is another blast from the whistle and a last triumphant chord from the band and the game is at an end.

The policeman announces a waltz then and the game-players move aside to let the dancers back on the floor.

Matthew straightens from the wall and takes his hands from his pockets with an air of decision. Dance? he says.

Can't, I say, tersely.

Why not? he says.

Don't know how, I say.

A waltz, says Matthew, his voice rising in derision. Any bugger can waltz.

I say, all right then, because I want so much to try, to be out there with the rest, under the Chinese lanterns, holding up my arms and tripping lightly across the floor to the sound of the band.

And so we walk out on to the floor and link ourselves in odd, awkward imitation of our elders, our young clasped hands old and heavy and out of place.

Then the music starts and my little black shoes that had felt so light and delicious are suddenly like the flat irons standing on the old range in the fat farmer's wife's kitchen.

I begin to stumble and drag behind Matthew and feel hot and confused. My feet won't seem to follow the music and I feel everyone is looking at me. But then Matthew begins to instruct in a clear, unhurried voice. Back, side, together, he says, pulling me with him to the rhythm of his quietly persistent chant.

His back, side, together, becomes like a spell, so that I wake up with surprise to find we have travelled the full length of the hall and are on our way back.

Two laps of the hall we have travelled before the dance stops, by which time Matthew has stopped chanting and I am swirling and rising and dipping unprompted and feeling like a princess.

We walk back to the wall to take up our slouching places again.

Where did you learn to dance? I ask.

School, says Matthew. Some school yours if they don't teach you to dance.

They do, I say.

Learn then, says Matthew.

Can't, I say again, almost whining, Can't, I say. And then, You know, lamely and trailing off.

Matthew whistles a little in the air and then looks down at his feet. I am too embarrassed to look straight at him, but out of the corner of my eye see the old look of scorn flit across his face followed by the old bemused shake of the head.

He frowns then and squinting up at a Chinese lantern says, not mockingly, but as if it was a matter of fact that needed to be stated, Still doing all that then?

I say, Yes, and then, You know, and then, Sort of.

Something about Matthew then makes me want to try to explain. I want to tell him about the texts and the testimonies, about the dream and the handshake and the stares. I want to tell him I'm not like him and I don't have his scorn. I want to tell him I'm frightened of not being saved but more frightened now of letting Him into my life. I know after waltzing with Matthew I don't care that I can't serve Jesus on the dance floor. I just want to dance.

I want to tell Matthew all this but I can feel the old tightening of the jaw and the lump in my throat. If I speak I know my voice will be cracked and shaky.

Thinking of all these things it seems to me the room has suddenly darkened. The lanterns seem to gleam a little less, the streamers to be less bright and gaudy.

Seeing again the foolish figure in the firelight and the text on the desk top brings pricking tears to my eyes so that I turn away a little more to the wall and blink them hard and fast.

I feel Matthew's curious eyes upon me. Digging his hands more firmly into his pockets, he seems about to speak when both of us are suddenly caught violently by the arms and pulled towards the centre of the room.

It is the policeman, dragging us away from the wall and pushing us forward for a game as he dragged us once as children out of other people's orchards and away from the fine, plump apples.

Matthew is not pleased for he is a young man now and much above silly games. I am not pleased either for there is still a lump in my throat and my eyes are still smarting with tears. But both of us know better than to try and disobey the Master of Ceremonies.

So, as the music starts, we walk around the chairs with the others, waiting for it to stop and sit down. Although we both want to be out, perversely there is always a seat for us both to drop down on to.

Soon we are only a handful, walking around the small clump of seats left. The music stops again and I am lowering myself carefully on to a chair when a boisterous little boy in grey flannel shorts and braces, who wants desperately to win, crashes his small but determined body against mine and on to the chair.

Uncertain on the new tiny heels, I rock dangerously and then collapse in a heap of dark dress and frothing net, one shiny shoe skittering across the floor to drop out of sight through a hole in the side of the stage.

I scramble to my feet, all skirt and net, and limp, red-faced and trying to pretend unconcern to the side of the room.

I lean against the wall trying not to cry and at the same time trying to work out how, when the game is finished, I can retrieve my shoe.

Suddenly Matthew is beside me, Matthew with dust on his smart new suit, a cobweb trailing over a shoulder.

The game is over and he has crawled beneath the stage to get the shoe which he is holding now in his large, freckled hands.

Pursing his lips and shaking his head, Matthew is mumbling about the foolishness of games. He bends down and, as I lean heavily against the wall, slips the shoe on my raised foot. It is a smooth and gentle movement, altogether a gesture that surprises me, one that does not seem to come from my understanding of what we are, Matthew and I.

I am silent then and confused, but the tears are gone from behind my eyes and I no longer want to cry.

But Aunt Esther is calling from the kitchen. Already a crowd of people is surging in that direction. I dart through them to get there first and slip behind the trestles to Aunt Esther's side.

By the time the swell has subsided I see by my watch that it is almost ten o'clock. I look out into the hall to say goodnight to Mikey and Corrie and Matthew but most of all to Matthew. There is no sign of Mikey and Corrie but Matthew is there. I see him standing, head bent and hands in pockets, in the middle of a laughing huddle of young men.

I slip away then, for times have changed and we are no longer children and I am too shy to say goodnight now to Matthew when he is grown up like this among his friends.

*

For some reason everything is better after the parish party. One day one of the girls in my class begins to chatter to me quite naturally as we bend over our work together. I look at her in surprise and then it dawns upon me that the incident of the

37

testimony and the text has been forgotten by all, except myself keeping its memory alive with my misery.

Yes, everything seems to be better after the parish party and when I look for a cause for this improvement it seems to have something to do with Matthew and his back, side, together, and with the music and the Chinese lanterns and the lost shoe.

I find I am thinking a lot about Matthew, which is strange because he has always been a part of my life and yet I have never had reason to think about him before.

Thinking about what happened at the parish party, it seems to me that while everything about us appears the same, something has changed.

It's true, of course, that Matthew is growing up and that being grown up goes deeper than the new suit and the pointed shoes. For at Easter he leaves school and surprises everyone by refusing to sign on at the factory along with the rest.

Instead he apprentices himself to a picture restorer which is considered odd in the village for now the factory is offering piece-work and overtime rates and fat wage packets and Matthew will make just a pittance cleaning up musty old pictures.

Strangely, only Uncle Ezra is on Matthew's side. I am serving beside Aunt Esther one day in the shop as a gaggle of factory wives gossip and sniff over what Matthew has done. But Uncle Ezra sticks out for him, shaking his head at the women and saying that Matthew is smart and Matthew will do all right and fat wage packets aren't everything.

Matthew goes to work on a new, bright blue scooter that pop-pops deliciously to tell me he's home. He takes Corrie on the back sometimes to deliver her eggs and he and Mikey go to the cinema on it on a Friday night, Mikey's face pasted all over with pleasure. And sometimes, when I'm on my way to the shop, he pop-pops up beside me and I jump on the back, feeling this strange new embarrassment as we jerk away and I cling on to his jacket, staring at the disturbingly intimate view of the back of his gleaming, coppery head.

Yes, everything is the same but somehow different. One

Saturday Matthew and Mikey and Corrie and me sit again on the barrel of Big Bessie, just for old time's sake. We sway and push to annoy, just like before, but for some reason the annoyance becomes real and the old tomfoolery explodes with new spiky flashes of anger. And with the spiky anger comes a new constraint, elusive and sad, like the scent of the honeysuckle on the sharp, early summer air, tantalizing and slipping away just as it is smelt, but remaining long in the nostrils and the memory.

We know that we have begun to separate, Mikey and Matthew, Corrie and me, begun to go our own male and female ways. We know that we can no longer go to the swimming stone together or to the orchard to steal apples or to the woods to swing on the old seat we put there so many years ago. We know that we cannot go and that while we cannot say exactly why, we know it has something to do with a new unspoken awkwardness which we cover up with the spiky irritation that bursts into anger.

It is like this then when Matthew pulls up beside me one evening when I am walking back from Aunt Esther's.

I clamber on to the back of the scooter, folding away my skirt, clinging on to Matthew, feeling the newness of it all. He takes off through the village. We pass my house and I am not surprised when we do not stop. For some reason I cannot explain I never expected tonight that Matthew would just drop me at the back gate as usual.

Inside my stomach something is fluttering delicately, something that could be alarm or pleasure. Whatever it is it seems to be working in concert with the breeze that raises goose pimples on my bare legs as we race along and pulls tendrils of hair from the rubber band at my neck.

We take the road to the swimming stone, pop-popping past the sagging farmhouse where I took tea with Aunt Esther and the farmer's wife. It is late May but the evening is still sharp and springlike. The sun is setting leaving streaks of pink clouds piled upon the horizon like the uplands of a distant, exotic country.

The road becomes rougher and Matthew steers the scooter carefully on the channelled and gullied surface, dry and hard after the winter wet.

Soon the road becomes a track which we ride along slowly till we come to a gate where we dismount. Matthew pulls down the stand on the scooter so that its handlebars swing round with a life of their own, like the head of an animal.

We climb over the gate and walk towards the swimming stone, pulling at blades of grass which we chew between bursts of staccato conversation, about school, about work, about the new, non-smoking young vicar who has announced his intention of giving up hearing the catechism from his young pupils each Wednesday morning.

Disappearing into the shade of the trees it is suddenly dark. Away from the light the pool at the foot of the waterfall is murky and opaque.

Sitting on the stone, our arms encircling our knees, it seems as though the place is asleep, so peaceful is it. Somewhere far away a cow lows and a tractor chugs gently. Unseen insects make soft plopping noises on the surface of the pool beneath us.

Looking down at the pool I remember with embarrassment the last time we had all been swimming there. Corrie and I were sunning ourselves on a bank in our knickers when Matthew and Mikey arrived unexpected. It was the first swim of the year and the winter had changed Corrie's shape. Mikey's eyes opened wide and his mouth dropped in surprise. Looksee, he said, with a little whistle of amazement. They'm pointed. It was the last time we went swimming together.

I shift slightly in embarrassment at the memory. Matthew breaks the silence. Why can't you dance? he says, pretending to concentrate on the job of dropping a stone into the pool below.

The water closes in over it with a long, hollow plop. You know why, I say. We're Brethren.

But why not? he persists. I mean why not dance, what's wrong with it?

We think, I hesitate, We think, it's not right. We think it's sinful. The word is old and foolish and out of place and I know it so I wait, unhappy and awkward for Matthew to break the silence again.

Finally he says, I never understood it. All that stuff about sin. That stuff about sin and second birthdays that your lot used to come out with.

I don't either, I say. I don't either. I never did.

Immediately, in one glorious moment, while the sound of my voice is still dying away in my ears, I realize I have spoken the truth. I realize I have never been able to make the connection between the innocent things that I desire and that dark, sombre word 'sin', that word that revealed itself to Uncle Ezra in the stinking, pitchy nightmare of the trenches and to my mother in the lonely shadows of the sanatorium.

It wasn't that I didn't want to believe and be saved, only that I couldn't believe in what I had to be saved from. My sin. The music and the dancing, the Chinese lanterns and the little tin of powder. All these things they wanted me to cast away. All these things I wanted to keep.

I don't understand it, I say again, repeating the words slowly and staring at Matthew, wide-eyed with my discovery.

I don't understand it, I say one more time, my voice beginning to rise in delight.

Chuck it then, says Matthew. Chuck it in then, he says, flatly and matter-of-factly. It can't be any good if you don't understand it.

For one wonderful moment, looking hard at Matthew, I think it really is that simple. That the decision can really be that flat and straightforward and matter-of-fact. I think that I can go home, like Matthew did after his first and only Sunday School and say, That's it. I don't want it and I'm not going any more.

But almost as soon as it is born, the belief dies, and I am shaking my head, amazed at my folly.

I see instead the impossibility of such an idea. Only a few seconds have passed and yet I see now quite clearly the absurdity of the thought that such a thing could happen, the absurdity of thinking that life could ever be different from the way it is. Worse, as the moments pass I feel a sense of panic that anything should change, that the web of belief, love, desire and fear in which I am caught and against which I struggle continually should suddenly disappear. I think to myself that this web is all I am, all I have, and that any other way of living belongs to others, like customs of a foreign land where I could only ever be a visitor.

I sit before Matthew, my arms still locked over my knees, a lump of miserable confusion. The light is dying all around me and in me too. I feel it sinking in my eyes as I stare at Matthew. Perhaps he sees it too, for he peers at me, leaning closer. His eyes are very blue and very near and I feel sad, very sad, so that my lips twitch a little and tremble.

Then Matthew takes my hand from my knees, gently surprising me, as he surprised me when he slipped on my shoe. He touches my fingers with his and says, Don't cry, softly and gruffly, as if he's afraid of the sound of his own voice in the still evening air.

He eases himself forward and bends his head, tilting it carefully on one side. Coming very close now, he presses his lips on mine, very softly and quite confidently, but also very quickly so that when he has pulled away I am half wondering if what he did, he did at all.

There is a moment then when everything seems to stop, when there is nothing but my eyes and Matthew's and my own wonder. And then something begins welling up inside me, something that absolutely must be the greatest feeling of happiness that I have ever felt.

As it rises it seems to spill out all over me, seems to race down through me to my very fingertips. I close my eyes momentarily with the pleasure of it and as I do so I hear the harsh sound of a work boot crushing soft spring grass and, immediately after it the strong, sharp, unwelcome syllable of my own name.

A dark shape stands in the archway of overhanging branches. It is my father.

*

Many times he took us there, my father, to the swimming stone, left us there, Matthew and I, tooting his horn as we waved our

42

sweets and our biscuits and lemonade in the air, to say goodbye. Many times he left us there to while away the hours, swimming and warming ourselves on the stones. But we were children then.

All aware that something had changed, I jumped to my feet, to stand in a new confused world overhung by guilt which appeared mysteriously, like a cloud out of an empty sky.

Matthew, for whom guilt was still an unknown, ambled slowly and easily to his feet, greeting my father with an interested, artless smile.

I turned away unable to look upon the scene. I went to the car, frightened and unprotesting as my father told me to, making my cowardly way back across the track to the scooter whose twisted head seemed to be straining to catch a glimpse of what was going on.

I could not hear what my father said to Matthew but I try to imagine it now, sitting beside my father in the old Morris as we chug slowly home. The pain that it causes, going over it in my mind like this, is so sharp as to be almost physical. It will never go away, this pain. Even when I go over the whole thing many years on. The pain is not for Matthew or for myself but for my father. Even now my eyes burn with tears of shame for him, at what he had to do, at what he had to deal with, all unprepared, all so unnecessary.

At home my mother is waiting at the ironing board in the kitchen, slamming the iron down on creases she smoothes and dampens with a cloth but does not see.

The kitchen is a new and awkward place, not the place I left, but a place echoing with outrage, where something new has entered in and from which something old and known and comfortable has fallen away.

Something beyond the boundaries of what we are has been attempted and the whole room accuses me. But what we are prevents me from being told of what it is I am guilty and the crime instead curls all around the three of us, shadowy and fearful and without a name.

Because of it my mother trembles on the edge of tears,

43

fumbling for the right thing to say. She cannot accuse me or express her horror and fear because she cannot find the words she needs and she cannot find the words because she does not know them.

And so her face works in an agony of hurt and frustration and she tightens her grip upon the iron trying at the same time to get a grip upon the words and phrases that elude her.

Eventually words stumble out unsatisfactorily. She speaks slowly and stiffly, as if in a language not her own.

She says, You are far too young to have a boyfriend. You will not be allowed to have a boyfriend until you are seventeen. You may not go out again in the evenings until you can be trusted. Now go to your room.

These are not the things she wants to say. She wants to say, How could you, Why did you, What did you do? What do you know?

Her hurt is deeper than mine. This word 'boyfriend' insults us both but it offends her too and causes her pain merely to use it. It taints her with the mark of the world to which it belongs, the world she does not understand and only waits in.

But I am not innocent like her and I love the word even though it surprises me. Who would have thought of Matthew as my boyfriend? Certainly not me. But now the word makes me think again of that feathery but firm mothwing of a kiss.

Later, sent to bed like a child, I begin to think like a woman. I think I would give anything in the world to have that kiss over again. I think there is nothing I would not give. I would give everything we are. I would give my soul.

*

Nothing is ever quite the same again after what happens with Matthew. What has fallen away from our lives is innocence and what has entered in sexuality, unspoken and sinister and disturbing the wall texts, the hymn books and the Bibles with its awkward, unexpected presence.

My parents now must grapple with the discovery that I am no longer a child and, worse, that I show the first unhappy signs of not growing up the way they would wish. By the Grace of God I have been saved from taking a bite from the apple, but who can forget that I reached up to the tree to pick it.

Sometimes I catch my mother looking at me, a sad, confused look upon her face.

Once a farm labourer talking to my father in the kitchen jokes with me.

He winks and says he wishes he were twenty years younger and as he says it my mother's back stiffens as she bends over the sink and my father glances at me, unease creasing his face.

I go to my room then without being sent. The embarrassment, the awkwardness between us, the unspoken, unnamed horror all point to my guilt and now I believe it myself.

Preachers straining from the pulpit begging me to be saved could not convince me of my guilt or the elders standing at the door, staring down into my soul. How is it then that Matthew has done it?

Not long afterwards a heavy, middle-aged builder, working upon our house, pushes me against the wall as I pass and dropping on to his knees as if in worship, buries his round, friendly face into my skirt and into my body beneath. I go to my room again, confused but feeling responsible somehow for these new wickednesses around me.

I begin to spend long hours in my room. Here, alone and dreaming in the window-seat. I build a new world, a new world of magic and romance, free from the guilt and confusion of the world outside.

I never see Matthew now for he has taken lodgings near his work. For a while I think I am heartbroken and weep a lot. But soon Matthew is just a shadowy figure in my new dream world and then I forget about him altogether.

I shall think of him one day, though, many years on. I shall remember him one humid early morning in a foreign country.

I shall think of him, my head still thick with the night's excesses. I shall think of him as I try and find a cab, as I try to make sense of an existence that leaves me empty and alone like this, in this damp, depressing daybreak.

Trying to make sense of everything in the back of the taxi, lurching as we turn a corner, a little sick from the heat and the smell of petrol and plastic, I shall find myself to be morally awash, my life devoid of touchstones, devoid most of all of the touchstone of guilt.

And then I shall think of Matthew and how they saved me from him, from nice, moral Matthew who worked hard and wooed and won the boss's daughter, Matthew the managing director, the chairman of committees and charities, who returned to the village with his lovely wife and handsome children, to settle there, its church warden, its parish councillor, its most successful and well-respected son.

3

Two years have passed. Now I am fifteen. Soon I shall give my testimony for the third and final time.

The older I have grown, the more I imagine I can detect in those around me a pressing concern for my soul. I think I feel it in the farewell handshake at the door, think I see it in the eyes of my mother and Uncle Ezra each time there is a conversation or a baptism in the Hall.

Those I have grown up with, sat next to at Sunday School are making their way through the waters of baptism and I know I must follow them. I must be baptized to save me not from my sin but from the questioning handshakes and the prying eyes that demand to know the state of my soul.

Yet the days pass and the weeks and still I cannot bring myself to ask for my baptism. In the end Cousin Arthur does it for me.

Cousin Arthur is not my cousin at all but I call him so, his being a friend of the family, but too young and jovial to be called 'uncle'.

I first meet Cousin Arthur when I am five. I serve him porridge and fall immediately in love with him. He leads a group of young men on a Christian camping holiday. They pitch their tents in a field close to my home. They build camp fires, sing choruses and give testimonies just as I should do one day.

Each morning the dozen or so of them take breakfast in our house seated at long trestle tables laid out in the sitting room.

They fill the place with the sound of their laughter and their jokes. My mother, young and pretty, stands pink with pleasure before the stove in her bright cotton dress, flushed at the heat but also at their chaste and deferential Christian admiration.

For two weeks I devote myself to Cousin Arthur, trotting around after him, demanding to be allowed to stay up late to hear him play the old pedal organ.

I have an image of him still, his feet working the pedals, his hands upon the keys, swaying his body backwards and forwards with the exertion, surrounded by healthy, red-faced young men, singing lustily, the sweat standing out upon their foreheads, the buttons straining on their white nylon shirts.

I adore Cousin Arthur and come in cutely every morning carrying his bowl of porridge, laying it before him, an offering before a god.

When I place it upon the white cloth he turns his bright blue eyes on me, creasing his suntanned face into a smile. Then he places his hands together and says grace out loud for the whole table while I, sitting upon a little stool at the end of the room, peep at him through my fingers admiring his fine, handsome face and his fair, crinkly hair. Oh, how I am betrayed by Cousin Arthur.

So much has changed when Cousin Arthur comes to tea ten years later. My early devotion has been replaced by fear. For I remember now that Cousin Arthur is a Fisher of Men and that he saved some half a dozen of the lusty young men during the fortnight's holiday and I think Cousin Arthur will almost certainly be out to save me too.

Ten years on Cousin Arthur's eyes are still a piercing bright blue and his hair is still fair and wavy. He is handsome still, too, and has lost none of his vigour and good humour.

When he preaches Cousin Arthur likes to say the Christian life is not a dull one. He likes to tell his would-be converts that they will not be giving up anything when they take Christ as their saviour but will be gaining much, much more.

Cousin Arthur likes to tell them that the Christian life can be fun and, as if to make the point, he makes little jokes so that we who are old hands at his game laugh quietly and knowingly, look at each other in pleasure or click our teeth as if to say, Of course, I understand, my goodness though, a joke, just fancy, in the message, my he's a rum one that Arthur.

Among the young Arthur is something very special, not just because he makes us laugh but because he is a genuine convert. For Cousin Arthur lived a Life of Sin before he was born again. Cousin Arthur was a commercial traveller who Drank and

Smoked and Did Other Things which he now will only hint at which disappoints the younger of us.

Cousin Arthur is still a commercial traveller but now instead of drinking and smoking and doing other things in the evenings he tries to convert the other travellers in his lodging house. He taxes them with the state of their soul across the liver and bacon and leaves tracts beside his bed for the next occupant. They say that Cousin Arthur cuts a swathe for Christ wherever he goes and his route each week can be traced by the trail of converted souls.

Certainly it's true that Cousin Arthur has a certain lustre compared to the average preacher and there were those who were surprised when he married grey-haired zealous Eileen with her serious air and quiet ways. Not least among the surprised were the other unmarried sisters in Cousin Arthur's meeting, younger and prettier with smarter hats than Eileen, who had thought her to be last in line for the favours of the popular and handsome preacher.

But now Cousin Arthur is sitting opposite me with Eileen at his side, taking tea before preaching at the Evening Meeting.

As for me, I am so frightened of him that I am having difficulty forcing down the multi-coloured trifle and the thin-cut bread and butter we always give our preachers before their meeting.

I am nervous and sweating for fear of Cousin Arthur's bright blue eyes. I fear that they will fix on me and that he will tax me across the table as he does his fellow travellers and he will ask me, How is it with you, Maud? How is it with your soul?

And so I keep my eyes on my plate and on my trifle and do not raise them, even to ask for more tea.

Just when I think the agony may be over, when I think I may have got away with it, when I think Cousin Arthur must be about to push his chair back and get up from the table, he tells us all the Sunday School is short of teachers.

Would you not like to teach in Sunday School, Maud? he asks, holding my eyes with his own, ice-blue and unblinking.

I realize then, meeting those eyes for the first time properly,

49

there never was a chance with Cousin Arthur, not Cousin Arthur who has lived a life of sin and who now makes up for it by saving the rest of us.

I am not baptized yet, I say.

Have you not taken the Lord? asks Cousin Arthur, sternly for once and unsmiling, wiping a last piece of trembling trifle from the side of his lips with a paper napkin.

Yes, I say, quite firmly considering the state of my mind and stomach which are both quivering to every corner with a complicated mixture of shame, embarrassment and disgust.

Yes, I say again, When I was eleven.

I glance at my mother for confirmation but she is turning away to pour out a last cup of tea. But it is enough for Cousin Arthur. And why should he disbelieve it? Why should it not be true? Perhaps my mother believes it and is turning away to hide her delight. My father is smiling and he believes it. Cousin Arthur and Eileen are smiling. Perhaps they all believe it. Perhaps it is true.

Now Cousin Arthur is telling me I must be baptized and I am saying, yes. He is telling me that, just by chance, he has been asked to see Uncle Ezra that very evening to fix another baptism and that I can be baptized at the same time. How lucky. How convenient.

Then Cousin Arthur says we must thank the Lord for Maud's salvation. He rises to his feet, and, leaning his knuckles upon the table begins to talk conversationally to God while we bow our heads. He thanks him for saving Maud so early, for saving her early on from a Life of Sin like his, for saving her from so many wasted years. And then he promises God Maud's young life, her bright young life, in His service. Amen.

That evening I scarcely hear a word of Cousin Arthur's message. The feeling of finality which descended on me when Cousin Arthur gave my life away has oozed throughout my body and is now weighing it down with its misery.

Sitting beneath Cousin Arthur in the pulpit, I can feel the trifle lying like a lump of lead in my stomach. My mouth is dry and my breath acrid from fear, from the dread of what is still to come.

Panic is a cramped pain inside me. I feel so weak I think I cannot stand and finding myself on my feet for a hymn, I am surprised and nervous, thinking I must collapse at any time.

Only once does Cousin Arthur break in on my misery, my fear and my panic. He leans towards me with a message specially for me. He says, the Christian life need not be a dull one, Oh No. And he rolls the, Oh No, off his tongue, bowling it in my direction, shaking his head and smiling a knowing smile that shares with me an understanding of the folly of the world that thinks the case to be otherwise.

And he tells me then about his Life of Sin, of how he Drank and Smoked and Did Other Things, but it only made him unhappy and wretched. And he tells me of the night that he cast himself in his sinful state before the Lord and was saved, to a new life, to a life of service, but not a dull life. A Christian life can be fun, repeats Cousin Arthur looking at me and smiling.

In their seats, the meeting nods appreciatively, pleased at its own good fortune at being able to hear the truth about the broad way and the narrow way from one who has had the chance to compare.

At the end of the service I collect the hymn books as usual but they keep slipping from my fingers and crashing to the floor.

Once I knock over a chair that falls with a clatter on to the lino, making the elders standing in a semi-circle around Cousin Arthur at the back of the hall, turn in surprise.

I smile at them weakly, knowing they are talking about me and stand the chair back up, returning it to its place.

Now Cousin Arthur is beckoning me so that I must take the long walk up the Hall to the threatening semi-circle at the end. I feel all their eyes on me as I walk towards them and I am terrified.

When I reach them my hand is grasped in Christian joy six times. Six times I and my soul are blessed so that I must stare six times into six pairs of eyes and must smile confidently six times as if I am at peace with myself and my soul.

Standing in the centre of the huddle I feel myself to be surrounded by a group of dark-suited, nodding archangels. I feel exposed and vulnerable, stripped to my foolish female soul. I feel like a prize, like a slave being sold into captivity. I feel all soul, nothing but soul, as though my soul had been removed and the rest of me discarded. I feel unimportant, as though this part of me that matters so much to them had been prised from me, to become their concern and their property, leaving me, the me that was left, a shell, hollow and incomplete.

Meanwhile the archangels are consulting their diaries and their black books. They are giving me a date. Uncle Ezra is shaking my hand, formally, as though we do not know each other. He is saying he will baptize me. I am mumbling my thanks, frightened and horrified, trying to look pleased and grateful.

Outside a car horn sounds. I say, My father, sharply, and then Good night, once, to all of them, turning before it has left my lips and slipping through the departing cluster at the door, quickly, before they can speak.

It is someone else's car, not my father's, but I keep on running. I run down the side of the hall, down the long narrow alleyway leading from the street light into the dark.

I run until I reach the end, to the entrance of a deserted crumbling warehouse.

And there in the pitch dark, all alone and away from all eyes, I throw up my trifle in one violent, wracking vomit.

*

Some nights in the meeting I can feel their love washing all about me in a warm, choking tide. I can feel it lapping, rising higher and higher, threatening to drown me, threatening to close its waters tenderly and relentlessly over my head.

And then I grasp hold of the chair in front of me as if this alone can stop me sinking, as if this alone can stop me being swept away in the treacherous current of their love.

I tell myself then that I will not sink, that I will not be dragged down. Instead I will walk upon the wicked waters of their ocean of redemption. I will walk and run and bound up into the clear bright air far above their lapping sea of love and far, far too

52

above the reaches of the bloody-browed stranger, he who stretches across the waves to me with that hand, that hand that goes on for ever, tap, tap, tapping on the door of my heart.

*

The gentle, delicate and uncertain privacy of my soul has been invaded.

My baptism seems to me a humiliation. I have been filled with this feeling of shame since the elders and Cousin Arthur stood nodding around me, exposing me with their loving concern for my soul.

It feels now as though that soul has been ripped away from me, to be exhibited in triumph at my public degradation.

I think I may as well go naked into the pool for, in truth, naked is the way I shall feel.

My unhappiness increases when I discover the other person to be baptized is a girl from my school.

Ruth is everything I am not, a wise virgin, studious, with a permanent half-frown upon her face as though something of importance always preoccupies her. She wears her religious separateness with dignity. She is pretty in a simple, unaffected fashion, a prefect and popular with everyone, even the spider-legged, sarcastic gym mistress. For Ruth is even good at games.

I cannot bear the thought of sharing the baptism waters with this saintly creature. I feel the first stirrings of fear about what I am about to do. At first I tried to convince myself that it might be all right. I might be saved. But then I gave up. It was hopeless. I knew the real state of my soul.

For as long as I can remember I have known about the unforgivable sin – a mysterious wickedness so evil as to be unpardonable, the one black spot that cannot be washed away by the rich, red blood of the Lamb.

No one ever says what it is for no one really knows. And now I am frightened. Now I fear my foolish, pathetic little piece of deception, my passing through the waters of baptism unsaved, may be that dreadful un-named sin.

I long to ask someone what they think the sin may be but I

fear to do so in case they guess the reason for my question. I think there is no one I can ask and then I see Ruth with her half-frown and her wise virgin air and I decide I will ask her.

I sign up for extra hockey which I loathe to try and catch her alone. One evening, legs bruised and aching and fingers tight with cold, I shamble back behind her to the gym.

I keep pace with her, action for action, garment for garment, as she showers and dresses. She packs her kit into her bag and puts on her pale pink, slightly upswept glasses. As she makes for the door I leap ahead and hold it open.

She smiles at me vaguely and walks through. I pass through behind her and closing the door behind me, call to her down the cold, echoing corridor, Excuse me, I'm going to be baptized with you.

She turns in surprise and as I walk up to her says, Good, briskly, then holds out her hand in a formal, ungirlish fashion.

I begin to talk to her, gabbling and letting go her hand slowly. I tell her about myself and my meeting. I say what a pleasure it will be to be baptized with her. She smiles, bemused, and I see her beginning to edge slightly away.

Her obvious desire to get away from me destroys what little confidence I have. I hear my voice, charmless and gauche, and almost instantly the rush of words dries up.

She says, Well, then and smiles again and turns to go. But I will not let her leave without me. I begin to walk along beside her, asking her about herself, about her meeting.

As she talks I try to plan how I will introduce the subject of the unforgivable sin, casually, in passing. I see it will not be easy especially since Ruth's legs are longer than mine and I am having to half run beside her to keep up with her.

Panting a little I hear a bus rumbling behind us. Ruth turns, and seeing it to be hers, begins to run calling goodbye over her shoulder.

I panic then. I can think only of getting an answer to my question so that just as Ruth has stretched a hand out to the pole on the platform and has pulled herself up I bellow out to her, What's the unforgivable sin?

Ruth turns along with the bus conductor and most of the people on the bottom deck. Even the bus driver is looking round, seeming loathe to drive away as everyone looks on in surprise. Then Ruth steps back off the bus platform and waves the bus ahead.

As it grinds away, the heads of the conductor and his passengers still turned towards me, Ruth walks back to my side.

The unforgivable sin, I say. I just wondered what it was. A preacher preached it last week, I go on hastily, and no one seemed to know what it was. And I just wondered, that's all. The Bible doesn't say, you see, and I just wondered.

My words dwindle away as Ruth peers at me through the lightly winged spectacles.

No, it doesn't say, she says, So why worry? If it doesn't say, why worry about it?

Oh I wasn't, I say. No, I wasn't worried. I just wondered, you see. I mean, I just wondered.

It doesn't matter anyway, does it? said Ruth. I mean if you're safe in the arms of Jesus you aren't going to commit it anyway, are you. He wouldn't let you, would he?

No, no, of course not. It was just that I wondered, with it being unpardonable and everything. I just wondered that no one knew what it was, that was all.

Actually, says Ruth, surprising me then, I always thought it was something simple anyway. She pushed her glasses on a little more firmly and looked at me almost defiantly.

I've heard a lot about what it's supposed to be, like devil worship and all that. But actually I think it's more likely to be something quite simple, like not caring, or not loving enough, or being cruel. I think a lot of things they say about it are rubbish.

I look at her quite shocked. I've never heard anyone suggest that something the elders said was rubbish and now, in front of me, this girl only a couple of years older than myself is saying it. Dismissing something the elders take seriously so easily, so matter-of-factly like this.

I'd forget all about it if I were you, says Ruth.

Oh, I will, I will, I say, still a little shocked at what I have heard but with a new feeling of hope swelling up inside me.

Forgetting the fear, I begin to feel almost joyful. Inside me the hope is turning to something else, admiration for this girl, adoration, love.

I hold out my hand to her, as she had done to me, thinking she is quite one of the best people I have ever met, thinking too that if there is any chance at all, I should like to be just like her.

For I know Ruth would not forget to bring extra oil with her lamp. Ruth would not be lost among the silks and satins of the market place.

No. Ruth will be there behind the closed oak door while I am on the outside. Oh, how I long to be a wise virgin just like her.

*

Sometimes though I think that in my foolishness lies my salvation. It makes no sense, of course, but deep in my heart I think I have an arrangement with God. I tell myself he won't let me burn. He won't cast me out with the rest. He won't leave me behind. When he sees me there, waiting below alone and forlorn, he'll weaken. The great God will weaken. And there in that last mighty moment, on the edge of eternity, he'll reach down and pick me up and take me, along with the rest, into glory. Because he knows me. And he knows that I'm weak and I'm tempted and easily led. And I know him. And I know he's a sucker for fools. We know each other, my God and I. And why not? Thrown together like this as we have been all these years.

*

And now Ruth is sitting beside me, praying privately, her head bowed. It is the Sunday evening before the baptism and we must give our testimonies. It is the third time I shall give my testimony and this time, it will be the last.

Several times during the weeks that have passed I have seen Ruth looking at me curiously. Once in a corridor she seemed to want to speak but I pretended not to have seen her and hurried away. For I do not want to talk to Ruth now.

My head is bowed too but I am not praying, pleading a little in anguish and fear perhaps, but not praying. Let me remember the things to say, God let me remember the words. All day I've been rehearsing them, like an actress. And now I'm sick with nerves before the performance and so choked with terror that I cannot sing the hymns.

Ruth is up on the platform speaking. She reads from her Bible, her text marked with a coloured bookmark and then closes it with a quiet snap, standing with it clutched in her hands before her, penitential and dignified.

Ruth is telling us that she was brought up in a Christian family for which she is truly grateful. But then one day she realized that this was not enough. She realized she had never truly surrendered her heart to Christ. And so she did so. There in her bedroom at home, she got down upon her knees and gave her life to Christ.

Now she knows the true blessing of belonging to him.

Ruth does not need war or disease to be saved. Ruth is not like Maud and the meeting that thrills to the tale of Cousin Arthur's salvation from a life of sin, now sighs in delighted unison at this evidence of another, encouragingly simpler way to the cross.

Yet something seems odd to me and pondering on what it could be I find it to be the sound of Ruth's voice floating down from the pulpit and the sight of the slim, female form standing in this sturdy, most masculine of battlements.

The women's meeting, where Aunt Esther took me occasionally as a child, groups itself in a circle on the blue lino beneath the pulpit, their speaker standing up in their middle to preach.

I realize I have never seen a woman in the pulpit before. I am marvelling at the oddness of it when I feel a soft touch upon my arm and find that Ruth is now back beside me and is telling me, with this gentle prod, that the meeting waits upon me.

And now I, instead, am in the pulpit – a woman, a girl, looking down on those I have known all my life, wondering how they do not know that I should not be here, how they do not know, these people who have watched every flicker of my

57

spiritual life since I first scribbled on Aunt Esther's pad, how they do not know that this testimony I am about to give is a fraud.

Perhaps my mother guesses. She is not looking at me. From the corner of my eye I can see her seated behind the organ, staring fixedly ahead at the open hymn book on the music stand, her hands folded in her lap. I think she does not want to look at me.

Aunt Esther will not meet my eyes either, but I suspect for different reasons. A reflective, regretful look is upon her face as she stares at a point on the blue lino beneath the pulpit.

Only my father looks up at me, love and encouragement beaming from his eyes. As I begin to speak his chin nods very slightly at each of my words as if he must work with me to force the words out.

For I am frightened up here in the pulpit, so frightened that for the first time in my life I am beginning to stutter, just as he does.

In the back of my throat I can feel the creeping tightness. I can feel the lock beginning its strangle hold on my jaw. I fight them both. I clear my throat, raising my chin and swallowing hard.

Looking up, I stare out over the meeting. And then I begin. I say that they have known me since I was a child. I say they have known me since I scribbled on the pad Aunt Esther used to bring for me at the evening meeting.

They smile at this and their smiles give me confidence. I say that although they have known me since I was a child only God really knows us. Only God sees all, I say, only God looks down into our hearts.

They shift slightly in their seats with interest and their interest makes me audacious.

I say that I was saved when I was eleven. I say it boldly, looking at them these people who should know it is not true, daring them to contradict.

I say, I was saved when I was eleven. I told my mother, I say. I was saved one night, after the meeting when, young as I was, I realized I had sinned and needed a saviour.

I say, I went home that night and could not sleep. I say I lay awake, staring into the dark, frightened and worried. And then, I say, I closed my eyes, and there, lying in my bed, I whispered out into the night, Jesus Save Me. And then, I say, I felt his peace, that peace that passeth understanding, flooding over me.

But then, I say, I became older and as I became older I became a backslider. I slipped off the narrow way, I say, on to the broad, because I wanted life to be exciting. I wanted other things.

I let my tongue drift gently over the 'other things' and I pause and then I say, But I was wrong, Oh I was wrong. All these things are worthless, I say. I realized that a short while ago. And when I realized it I pledged myself anew, gave my heart to Him again, begged Him to come in a second time.

And now, I say, I want to live for Him. I want to live for Him alone. I want the narrow way, I say. I want the Christian life. I grasp the lectern then with both hands, as the preachers do, daring anyone to say it is not so, this thing that I say. I say, I know it now. The Christian life need not be a dull one.

And then I relax my grip from the lectern and stand back.

Humbly and quietly I say, I know my name is written in the Book of Life. I know I shall be there with you, the saints, around the throne. Not for me the Lake of Fire, I say, not for me.

There will be no night there, I say. No hunger. Or thirst. And no more weeping.

It will not be long now, I tell them. See the wickedness, the ungodliness. The time is at hand.

Till then we wait, I say. Till then we wait. Watch and pray, I say. Watch and pray.

Only a little while, I tell them. Only a little while.

*

Aunt Esther gives me a white nylon overall from the shop to be baptized in. She also gives me an exquisite Bible with shiny, ivory covers, the sort of Bible brides carry on their wedding days with a posy of flowers. A highly unsuitable Bible for a baptism, a most unBrethren Bible, without a column of references and translations slicing heavily and formidably down the centre of each page. I love it and disconcert my mother by stroking its smooth and gleaming covers. I take it with me to my baptism.

I change into the overall in the toilet, listening to the sound of the kettle boiling merrily outside on the gas ring.

I stand in the hot, steamy kitchen, embarrassed and undignified in the too-long, too-large overall, watching silently as one of the women busies herself with cups and milk and sugar.

Then the door opens and there is Ruth. Her brown hair always shining and shifting gently against her cheeks when she speaks is plastered now to the side of her head. Beneath the drips, she peers at me myopically and a little foolishly so that I realize suddenly that the serious half-frown habitually upon her face which I have so much envied is not evidence of some matter on her mind but of the fact that she is hopelessly short-sighted.

She slops past me to the toilet and as she passes gives me a wan, almost unhappy smile that strikes terror into my heart. If baptism can do this to Ruth, what can it do to me?

But it is too late for such fears. An elder is opening the door and I am walking past him, through the little entrance lobby and into the hall.

The meeting is singing as I wait at the door. They turn their eyes from their hymn books to look at me, to smile at me, encouraging and welcoming.

I begin to walk along the long line of lino between the chairs to the corner of the room, to the corner which has haunted me for so many years, to the pit which I have felt beneath my feet for so long.

Not for me the bottomless pit but this one now, open and waiting, full of water and steaming slightly around the figure of Uncle Ezra, waiting for me now with open arms.

A feeling of horror, rich and raw, steals over me. Disgust begins to shake me from head to toe and makes me hesitate on the top of the steps.

My legs seem to be made of lead they are so heavy. I think they will not take me down into the water. Around me the meeting waits. Ahead of me a look of faint surprise is flitting across Uncle Ezra's face as I stand motionless above the water.

And then a shutter seems to snap down across my brain. Something inside me seems to click itself off and I see as I look down one leg and then the other carrying me down the steps and into the water. I see an elder's hand touch my arm to steady me but I feel nothing.

It seems to me that my body has turned itself into a hard, protective outer shell, so that this touch and the water creeping now up to my waist and even the grasp of Uncle Ezra as he takes my hand cannot reach the soft and private place inside me.

I can see the large white overall billowing up around me and my hands pushing at it frantically, trying to keep it down, but I feel nothing. I, Maud, who has lived in fear and loathing of this event, now seem entirely separate from it.

And it is in this moment that I suddenly see it all to be true, that I realize how right they all are, all those people around me, to be concerned only for my soul.

I see their wisdom in being concerned only for this most precious part of me and I see it all so clearly that I want to turn to them, here in the water, and hold out my arms to them in an embrace of their rightness and their love.

Particularly I want to hold out my arms to my mother and to say to her, I understand, of course, the soul. How could anything be more important than this?

I want to say to her, I understand now why you did it. I respect you for it. I love you. But you've lost.

For in the same moment that I feel the blinding sense of separateness of mind and body, I feel too with equal certainty that my soul is still my own and always will be. And I never know and feel it more than several seconds later when I step, unashamed and unafraid into Uncle Ezra's red and brawny shopkeeper's arms, to be slipped quickly, quietly and efficiently in and under the waters of baptism.

*

Afterwards they said I must have caught a cold. They said no matter how hard you tried, turning up the heating, waiting

61

with the warm towels and tea, there was always the chance of it. You couldn't really guard against it, they said.

They said all this after I am found shivering and weeping in the toilet when the baptism is over.

Walking awkwardly back through the water to the steps I feel weak not with the effects of the water but with the enormity of my discovery that my soul is my own and that no one can take it away from me.

I feel deliriously happy and raise my hand to the elder who waits at the steps in friendship before he has time to put out his own.

My eyes are still bleary from the water and my hair is sodden, but my happiness is rapturous as I set out from the steps to walk back through the congregation.

I feel a desperate need to share my joy with those I love most dearly, feeling as I do that I now understand what they are and what they have been doing for the first time.

So it is that drawing level with my parents I slow my steps a little and then, as they both look up from their hymn books, I turn upon them a look of the most radiant ecstasy.

And so it is too that, restored to my everyday clothes and passing among the congregation with Ruth to receive pious good wishes, I overhear my father saying to my mother in a voice, happy but faintly puzzled, Didn't she look happy?

Which gentle and sincere expression of love blots out my rapture at a stroke and replaces it with regret, wretched and hopeless.

In a moment my triumph becomes my bitterest defeat so that I stop mid-handshake and feeling the tears starting, run headlong for the toilet. Which is where they find me later, shivery and feverish and a little weepy and why they think that I must have caught cold.

*

Is this the Unforgivable Sin then, not washed in the Blood of the Lamb but sipping its remembrance?

I wonder this the next Sunday morning, shifting restlessly in my seat, my gaze fixed on the white cottage loaf on the silver plate, the tall, lidded jug and the empty chalice.

For as long as I can remember I have sat here each Sunday morning, catching tantalizing glimpses of the divine liquid, shining in its chalice.

I have watched as the men press its stain from their lips with their handkerchiefs and the women flutter its mark from theirs with scraps of white lace.

More and more I have wanted to reach for the chalice as it passes before me from my mother's hand to Aunt Esther's. More and more I have wanted to steal a sip of this bloody red liquid. The desire for the wine is as strong and as dark as its colour and if I should not be here at the Lord's Table, or if this be the Unforgivable Sin, no matter. I shall have my wine.

On this morning, the first since my baptism, when each devotion should be so special to me, the hymns seem more dull and doleful than usual, the prayers more tedious and meandering.

After what seems like a taste of eternity, an elder rises to his feet and moves to the table. He breaks into two and then four the crusty, bulbous loaf and prays over it. His prayer finished he takes a pinch of the bread for himself and then passes it to the person next to him, sitting down to continue his prayer in private.

So the bread passes around the Hall, bowing heads in prayer as it goes. Receiving it from my mother's hands, I feel for the first time a burst of pride, grown up and womanly.

Of course I should not be here. Yet none the less this silver plate and milk white loaf ushers me, publicly at least, into a new belonging, charges me with mysterious new rights and responsibilities.

Taking a peck of the loaf between my thumb and forefinger as I have seen everyone do for so long, I feel old and prim and settled. I place the peck between my lips. The crumb is light and foamy and almost without taste yet I am not disappointed. I pass the plate in pride to Aunt Esther and lower my head again, far too excited to pray.

Silence and anticipation ring in my ears as I wait for the wine. My desire has reached fever pitch. Out of the corner of my eye I see my mother watching, curious and frowning, as my fingers twist and turn a small lace handkerchief.

But now the elder has risen again and has flipped the top of the silver jug up and is now, even now, pouring out the lovely liquid in a rich and gleaming stream of sight and sound.

Again he prays and again, taking first for himself, starts this time, the cup, upon its journey. I ache with suspense as it passes from hand to hand, leaving in its wake the trail of bloodied lips. I lean forward tensely watching it, fearing for it. Oh, be careful. Do not spill it before it gets to me.

And now at last, here it is, before me. I turn and lift it from my mother's hands, holding it, reverently, almost paganly before me. And now I raise it to my lips and feel the liquid surge up from inside the chalice and into my mouth.

Oh, it is delicious, heavy and sweet, the first wine I have tasted, like nothing I have ever drunk before. I cannot bear to tear it from my lips. I want to take a great swallow and feel it rush down my throat and wash through my whole body.

But I have had my sip and now I must pass the chalice to Aunt Esther, which I do, reverently again, with both hands but with a look too of greedy, unholy longing.

I lower my head like the rest but not to pray like them, instead to savour the sweetness and richness of the taste.

But already something is wrong. The sweetness and the richness is disappearing and instead in their place comes a new sourness, an after-taste which may be the wine or the fetid aftermath of an over-satisfied anticipation.

A bitterness that started in my mouth has crept down into my very soul. It is soaking me now, oozing into every corner of my being, telling me all my delight was nothing, that all is hopeless, for all for ever now will be this crumb, this sweet, unsatisfying sip, this empty passing of the plate and cup between my mother and Aunt Esther.

All that needed to be done has been done now.

I have stood in the pulpit to give my testimony and no one

stepped forward from those I had known for so long to contradict me.

I have passed through the waters of baptism in Uncle Ezra's arms and have risen again, undetected.

And now, finally, I have drunk the wine and shall do so on and on now, for the rest of my life.

I am safe now from the handshakes and from the eyes that bored down into my soul. And now I am in despair. For I have found that the warmth of security cloaks an insidious and deadly dissatisfaction that the outcome of the struggle, the end of all the fear and the pain, should be this empty play-acting, this passing of the cup for ever from my mother's lips to mine.

I feel cheated, now, for her and for myself. Inside me now is an absurd, illogical yearning for a member of the meeting, an elder with accusing handshake and burning eyes, to rise from his seat and point a firm, uncompromising finger at my falseness.

But no one does and I know now with dreadful certainty that no one ever will. They have known me, these people, since I was a child. But only God sees all. Only God really knows us. Only God can look down into my soul.

4

The evangelist visits the town every year. He brings with him his tent which he and his helpers put up in a field on the outskirts of the town, on the road to our village.

He brings with him, too, his wife, who used to sing in opera, but now sings sweet songs of penitence and capitulation which tear people from their seats and brings them stumbling and surprised to the feet of her husband.

He stands upon the platform as they barge along the rows and to the front, weeping and awkward. He watches them, slapping the cord of the microphone behind him like a singer in a nightclub. Come, he tells them. People will let you through. And they do.

His eyes dart all about the tent watching them stream to the front until he closes them, his hands cupped in prayer around the microphone, shaking his head and moaning his thanks to the Lord.

Beneath him, on the floor, stands Uncle Ezra in the centre of a line of elders from meetings all around. Their heads are bowed and their hands folded over their Bibles as before them the group deepens with the shufflers, the scurriers, the slouchers, all making their way to the front.

They raise their heads sometimes the elders, neither smiling nor unsmiling, men of stone, fearing perhaps that to smile would be to disturb or to give something away.

They stand like retainers knowing all that is to be done will be done by Him and their part is just to take these lambs by the hand and lead them out of the marquee and into His Kingdom.

And they do, afterwards. They lead them to small tents around the back where they take them to corners to read and to pray so that afterwards, long into the summer twilight over the green, sweet-smelling field, comes the gentle murmur of hushed and halting voices.

Come, says the evangelist, Do not be afraid. We're here to help you.

Say, 'I will, Lord', says the evangelist, Here and now, this evening, this moment.

Take this step for Christ, says the evangelist, This one step to the front. Your friends will wait, says the evangelist. And they do.

Come just as you are, sings his wife. And they do, too, year after year, shifting at first uneasily from foot to foot, torn between going and staying, mouthing words they do not see, glancing nervously from side to side and finally, dropping their hymn books on the seats behind them and pushing their way to the front, apprehension and anticipation chasing each other across their faces.

When Uncle Ezra preaches he talks of sin, anonymous and mysterious, but the evangelist tells of drugs and drink and violence and death. And when the evangelist preaches he whispers and shouts. He pleads and cajoles and sometimes even weeps. For every soul in the tent lies upon his heart. Every soul that he wins is God's work, everyone that he loses, his failure.

The evangelist stays for a week.

Each night Uncle Ezra shuts up shop early to be there in the tent, before the meeting, praying for souls.

They pray for a miracle, he and the elders. They pray for revival. They pray to God to bless this meeting, this crusade, with many souls, now in these last days, with so little time.

He bothers me still, the evangelist, baptised as I am. I worry about what he could do.

Sometimes I think it will happen to me what happens to them, those others who stagger past their eyes wide with surprise at what they are doing.

Sometimes I think it will happen to me, so that I'll lurch past them, my legs taking me off, of their own accord, carrying me, relentlessly, helplessly, down the grassy green aisle to his feet.

*

It is at the evangelist's that I first see Frank. One night he edges his way in through the entrance at the back of the tent. I hand him a hymn book and he takes it but he does not see me. I see him, though, and later I take a seat near him the better to watch him.

He wears blue jeans, frayed at the bottom, dragging on the ground at the back and riding up at the front over scuffed and dirty gym shoes. Tucked into the jeans is a T-shirt so old and pale and well-washed that the design upon its chest is an elusive, indecipherable glimpse of what could be moons, or stars or strange, horned beasts.

He sits on the end of a row. I sit in the same row, opposite him, on the other side of the aisle. I cannot sit nearer for I am afraid that if I do I will stretch out and touch him.

For I have an urgent need to reach out and feel the slightness of his body where the softness of the faded T-shirt meets his waist. I have an urgent need to place my finger through the thin band of black wiry hair woven into a bangle at his wrist and to stroke the skin of the pale face, stretching it out gently with my fingers, away from the eyes of astonishing darkness which glittered out at me when he took the hymn book unseeing.

But most of all I have a need to take his head between my hands and to feel the silken softness of the jet black hair which falls to his shoulders undisturbed by wave or curl and which even now is dancing with light from the last long rays of the sun slanting through the tent door.

Tonight the evangelist whispers and moans. Tonight he shouts and shakes his fist. Tonight he even weeps.

All have sinned and come short of the glory of God, says the evangelist. All, he says, all, thundering his hand down hard upon the wooden lectern and making the microphone leap.

Jesus says I am the Way, the Truth and the Life, says the evangelist, jabbing his finger into the air as he speaks.

For God so loved the world, he says, He gave His only begotten Son. And he lingers lovingly then upon the strange, unwieldy, old-fashioned word as if in love and repeats it. Begotten he says, wonderingly, as if lost in it.

Behold I stand at the door and knock if anyone hear my call I will come unto them. Anyone, anyone, says the evangelist, his voice rising higher and then dropping to a low, comforting murmur. Anyone, says the evangelist.

Open the door, says the evangelist, loud and peremptory, and then, open the door, again, soft and begging. Open the door, he says, menacing now, taking the microphone from the stand and advancing towards us.

Let him into your heart, whispers the evangelist, Let him into your life. Come, whispers the evangelist.

And they do, from the side and from the middle, from the front and from the back. I dare not look at him now, this beautiful stranger. I dread the sight of him, slight and dark and walking unsteadily, all his glittering brilliance left behind with his hymn book on the seat.

We will pray for you, says the evangelist. And I do. I pray for him, this beautiful stranger, his image pressed hard upon my closed eyelids and stabbing like a knife in my chest. I pray for his soul, that he may keep it, that he may hold on to it. That he will not go to the front.

Come, says the evangelist.

Stay, prays Maud.

Do not say no, says the evangelist.

Do not say yes, prays Maud.

They are swelling all around us now. To my right there is a sharp movement. A hymn book snaps closed and slaps upon the seat. I look up in fear. He is moving from his seat while they smile all around him, smiles of Christian love and encouragement.

He is standing now uncertainly at the end of his row, shifting from foot to foot unsure whether to go or stay. On his face is a look of confusion as if he is trying to remember something. He is feeling now in the pocket of his jeans and is reaching down and sweeping from the grass a small crushed packet of cigarettes.

And now he is walking, briskly and easily, a small smile upon his face, along the soft green aisle to the entrance and out into the sweet, free summer night.

*

After that I pray for Frank a lot. I make pacts and promises with God.

Let me see him again, just once, and I'll do what you want me to. Let me see him just once and I'll be what you want me to be. Let me see him just once and I'll be saved.

Sometimes I am bolder.

Let me see him again and I'll lead him to you.

*

'Mister Frank' Jane calls him the day, several months later, when my prayers are answered.

She lingers derisively over the 'Mister', her hamburger pinched neatly between fine, slim, silver-ringed fingers, her elbows elegant upon the plastic-topped table.

Mister Frank, she says again, pointing a finger at his back as it retreats from us into the executive dining room, using it then to flick a long sweep of fair hair back behind a swaying earring.

Mister Frank, she says in answer to my question, slanting her velvet blue, black-rimmed eyes in mockery and pursing her smooth pink lips.

Earlier that day, still awkward in my new job at the factory, I had been sent with a query to one of the men on the juddering, chugging assembly line.

I was timorous and polite but despite this he rounded upon me in anger and burst into a storm of obscenity which seemed to me to sound the more harsh and violent for his strong foreign accent.

I was transfixed by the sound of the forbidden words, words I had heard before at school in corners but never like this, used seriously in anger. I watched in horrified fascination his lips moving, as if on a film speeded up, spewing forth the words and phrases.

I was so engrossed in the words, rolling them over in my mind, that I did not notice that the man had gone quiet and, along with the rest of the line, was watching me questioningly.

I was backing away, deeply embarrassed, when I trod upon a toe and turning, found it to be Frank's.

At first I did not recognize him. I had said a muffled Sorry into my chest and was scurrying back to the office before I realized that the young man in the dark suit with the neatly trimmed head was the same jeans and T-shirted stranger with the silky black hair.

Which is why I asked Jane who he was for I knew she would know.

Mister Frank, she says to me finally. The boss's son.

*

I am lucky with Jane. For Jane knows everything. They put me beside her the morning I arrive. They tell her to teach me the job and she does.

She teaches me how to file the mountain of invoices they bring to us each morning on a creaking silver trolley.

She teaches me not to work too hard so that some nights we must do overtime. She teaches me to smile at the studious looking bespectacled clerk who runs the factory drama society and to cut dead the flashily good-looking salesman who I smiled at, all unawares, on my first morning.

Jane teaches me other things too. She teaches me to draw a black rim around my eyes as she does to hers and in a small store room off the factory floor she tries to teach me, unsuccessfully, to smoke a cigarette. And tonight after work she will teach me the delights of the Rose and Crown – the first public house I have ever been in.

For today is Friday and snug in my purse are two crisp five-pound notes which I still cannot believe are mine.

Working at my desk at around noon I felt suddenly an air of tension and anticipation around me. I saw people look up from their work and lean back in their seats, turning to talk to their neighbours.

At the end of the factory floor a door suddenly opened and clanged shut behind a girl with a green tray balanced upon her hip. She tip-tapped towards us on high heels, swaying her wide skirt as she walked. Gold bangles upon her arm and large hoops at her ears jangled as she handed me my pay packet so that I felt as though I was being offered flowers or good luck charms from a gypsy.

Now back at my desk after lunch, I spread the notes out on the desk before me again in wonder. Then I reach nervously for the phone and dial a number hesitantly.

At the sound of my mother's voice I am suddenly afraid and have an urge to put down the phone. But instead I close my eyes and begin to talk.

Less than a minute later I replace the receiver.

I lean back in my chair and cross my arms, my eyes resting on the money. I am astonished at the simplicity of it all, that it was all so easy, telling my mother the lie and having her believe it.

I told her I must do some overtime to learn the job and that I should be staying late after work. I told her I would go to the Friday night young people's meeting straight from the factory.

There was a moment's silence then between us which seemed as I waited very large and empty and around which my lie seemed to clang and echo.

But then she just asked me what I would do about eating and when I said I would get a sandwich from the canteen she said she would keep my dinner warm. And then there was a click and she was gone.

Now, resting my eyes upon the money, I have a sudden vision of her at the other end of the phone, in a work dress, pins all over her chest with needles trailing cotton.

It causes me a sharp stab of pain. I collect the notes together to return them to my purse and reach for a pile of invoices.

*

Jane has passed all her exams and is working for a year before going to university. I have failed all mine which is why I am at the factory.

But sitting facing me, framed by the high back and arms of a settle in the Rose and Crown, she makes me believe I have been so much more clever and daring than her. Failing exams, she says, is so much more in-ter-est-ing, and she drags out the word, pulling her fingers through her long hair, tossing it away from her face and making her long thin silver earrings dance.

I agree with her, of course. For I agree with everything she says. I am two thirds of the way through a gin and tonic and the effervescent, perfumed liquid which I have never tasted before is making me feel wonderfully at one with myself.

Everything Jane says makes sense to me and I feel deeply gratified that such a clever person should have chosen me to be her friend.

I feel wonderfully warm towards her. I feel we are beginning an altogether new sort of friendship, deep and female and grown-up.

Jane says we must go to the city shopping when we have earned some extra money from our overtime. She says we must join the factory dramatic society because it will be doing Brecht and Jane says Brecht is good. She says I must come and stay with her for a weekend and meet her father, the reverend.

I smile at everything she says, humbly in delight, amazed that life can all of a sudden open up in this way.

Getting up to buy two more drinks, I find the backs of my legs strangely weak, not in any unpleasant way, but rather as if they were a little soft and the rest of my body, particularly my head, airy and light.

At the bar, watching the landlord press the glasses beneath the upturned bottles, my eyes which have begun to rove a little out of control, become transfixed upon a sign which tells me it is illegal for those under eighteen to buy alcohol.

Taking some coins from my purse I want to giggle that on top of everything else, I am now breaking the law.

The coins are made of quicksilver and run from my fingers, dropping on to the floor, clinking the brass foot rail as they fall.

I am scrabbling on the lino for them when I come across a neat, expensive black shoe and next to it another one, both joined, I find as I look up, to a pair of dark trousers.

Rising upwards from the floor I find the trousers to be followed by a jacket and on top of that a head which belongs to Mister Frank.

73

Standing beside him and juggling a pile of play books is the bespectacled clerk who, seeing Jane, makes a rush to her table, calling his order over his shoulder.

Confused at standing so close to my beautiful stranger I knock over one of my drinks. The clear liquid runs over the bar top and the landlord, reaching for a cloth to mop it up peers at me closely.

How old are you? he says.

Eighteen, I say, astonished at the firmness of my voice in this, my second lie of the day.

Amazing, says the landlord, Always eighteen.

My round, I think, says Frank, stepping neatly between me and the bar and fixing me with the same pair of glorious, glittering dark eyes that swept by unnoticing when I handed him the hymn book.

*

Later, sitting by his side, making gentle, sympathetic noises as he reveals to me confidentially the difficulties of being the boss's son, I feel like a player in a perfect drama.

The clear liquid that swirled around the ice cubes is swirling now around my body, seeping into every toe and finger.

Watching the other two discussing the play and hearing Frank's voice murmur a monologue in my ear, it seems to me I am myself acting one of a number of parts, perfectly written, or a piece perhaps in a perfect chess game, moved by an unknown hand whose finger I feel resting gently and meditatively upon my head.

I feel blessed and golden, among blessed and golden people, so that turning my face to Frank it seems to me that the soft words of encouragement I murmur are so fine and so perfectly formed that they ooze out between my lips like precious stones.

It is then that I see the clock above the bar that tells me the young people's meeting has been under way ten minutes.

I jump to my feet, reaching for my bag. Frank's monologue breaks off awkwardly and abruptly and his face looking up at mine is surprised and even a little hurt.

74

The other two look up, too. Baby-sitting, I say, brightly.

Twenty minutes later I sit tipsily and a little miserably upon the steps of the Hall. The last long gulp of gin and tonic seems still to be washing around inside me, even after my hot, panting run, making my brain spongy and fizzy.

Out through an open polished wood door comes the sound of a hymn, tentative and thin, sung by too few voices, without accompaniment.

It sounds vulnerable and rather pathetic and, drunk as I am, it makes me want to cry.

It is one of the old hymns, a gospel hymn, a hymn that wheedles, and begs and pleads, a hymn that searches for my soul.

It falters through the door, urging me to hear the Master's voice, urging me to see him watching and waiting, urging me to answer his soft and tender call.

It is the message I have heard many times before, but sitting upon the steps rather drunk, it seems for once quite new. I wonder if this can be my moment, if this can be my battlefield. My dark sanatorium night.

I close my eyes as the hymn swells to a warning that shadows are gathering and death may be coming. But instead of the soft, loving eyes of the Master I see a glittering pair of dark ones. I feel again the touch on my elbow that set all my skin on fire and hear, beneath the melody of the hymn, the strange, hypnotic sweetness of a murmuring voice.

Later, much later I open my eyes to find a fine rain is falling and has silvered all my clothes. It seems as though many hours have passed but when I look at my watch it is only ten minutes later.

The hymn has been replaced by a hum of voices, punctuated by the odd, clear innocent laugh.

I rise a little unsteadily to my feet. Behind me somewhere a chair scrapes upon the lino and I snatch up my bag from the steps in panic. I begin to run, along the road away from the Hall.

I run past the little shop where the widow once bought the tobacco, around the corner and away, out of sight of the group

75

of orderly, plainly dressed young people who presently come out through the doors, Bibles in hands, to face the damp drizzly night.

*

Every Sunday night the preacher tells me to lay down the pack of sin upon my back. Every Sunday he tells me the longer I delay, the heavier will grow my burden. And he is right. For day by day my sin is growing. My sin – the gaudy, worthless collection of things that I desire that are forbidden. This is the pack the preacher demands that I lay down before the cross.

And I do, sometimes. Sometimes I lay it down upon the grass, untie it and shake out the trinkets for one last look. They glitter and sparkle in the grass, brass and beads and glass. I lift them up and finger them, dangle them to catch the light. And then I gather them together and pack them all away, for I love them, these worthless oddments, this bric-à-brac, and I cannot bear to part with them.

Beneath the cross, on top of old Golgotha, I paint my face and dance and dream. I pour a glass of deep red wine and raise it at the cross. I raise it to the sorrowful dark eyes. My sin, I say, the glitter not the glory.

*

The result of the shopping trip with Jane is a black shiny mac cut rather shorter than I am used to, a tight black skirt and a purple blouse with ruffles at the neck and sleeves.

My mother approves of none of these things. Her disapproval though is curiously muted for a new and subtle alteration has come about in our relationship, a change that has all to do with money.

I feel it that first Friday I bring my wages home. Laying that first five-pound note upon her outstretched palm, I see a look of regret in her eyes, a look also of fear, but most of all one of surprise, surprise that giving birth could come so quickly to this.

In this look and in my understanding of it lies the beginnings of a dissolution.

The following Friday, pressing a second five-pound note into her hand, I tell her I am joining the factory drama society and therefore will be late home on Tuesdays and Thursdays.

I see her lips strain at the corners, but she says nothing, merely closes her fingers over the note and turns away, bending to place it in the old black handbag.

Watching her, I feel the triumph die within me. It is the handbag that does it, the old handbag with the story told a hundred times to anyone my mother discerned to be doubtful of the power of prayer.

She would tell them how when Maud was very small, the three of them, she, Maud's father and Maud, had gone away on holiday to a cottage by the sea. She would tell how they had run out of money half way through the week and how they had sat upon the rocky, pebbly beach and prayed, the two of them, Maud's mother and father, with Maud in her bonnet and sun dress patting sandcastles on the little strip of damp sand at the water line. And then she would tell how some time later, reaching into her handbag for a handkerchief to wipe Maud's nose, she found a five-pound note, lying, almost hidden, down the side pocket of the bag.

And so the little bag with its two handles and pointed knobs on the top, could not be thrown away even when it became old and shabby and instead was given a special place in the house, holding the housekeeping and the holiday money, like a relic with holy properties protecting us, preventing us from ever being that penniless again.

But now Maud has become the provider, not God. Her five-pound note lodges, half-hidden down the side pocket of the bag, not His.

I am in the drama group now, the prompter, sometimes a peasant. Afterwards on Tuesdays and Thursdays we go to the pub, Jane and Frank and I and the rest. On Mondays and Wednesdays Jane and I often do overtime for the factory is very busy. Sometimes afterwards we go to the pub. On Fridays, though, I go to the Young People's meeting, sitting, chafing, through the hymns and the prayers and the Bible quizzes. On

Sundays I go to the Hall, to the Lord's Table, and the Evening Meeting and the Bible Study afterwards. The week belongs to me but the weekend, still to God.

Sliding between the two lives, I think life may go on for ever this way and am too relieved to be dismayed, like someone involved in long and bitter hostilities, who is grateful for the truce, whatever the terms. I look at Aunt Esther, slyly, as I sit beside her, wondering if this is the way it will be for me, too, keeping the faith, but keeping faith too with the precious, private corners of my life.

I never wear the shiny black mac to the meeting or the neat little Sunday suit to work. Sometimes I feel like the cardboard doll I played with as a child, with an outfit for every occasion, clipped on to her shoulders with little cardboard flaps.

But then one Sunday morning, rounding the corner by the house in the car from the meeting, I see Frank's car with him at the wheel and Jane in the front seat.

They want me to go for a drive but I cannot. I make excuses. Relaxed in their jeans and their sweaters they eye curiously my neat Sunday suit. They drive off after my mother calls over the wall to me sharply that lunch is ready.

All day after their visit, I feel ill at ease and unsettled. The sight of their car waiting for me, as incongruous and out of place as their clothes and their plan for the day, plays over and over in my mind.

Their visit from the weekday world which we, all three, inhabit, is an intrusion upon the tight, private world of my weekends. The gentle, haphazard nature of their appearance breaches with ease the wall that I have erected between the two worlds and which I had thought to be impenetrable. It breaks the spell, sweeps the sleep from my eyes so that I can see clearly that the two worlds in which I live cannot be kept apart for ever.

In their curious gaze, in my mother's call over the wall I see the worlds already beginning to collide, already beginning to break up into too many and too small fragments for either to be patched up and put back together again.

Which is why, I suppose, I decide to take my parents to the play.

*

Many years on I am still appalled at my own callousness in insisting that they come. They do not want to. They know they will be hurt and, seeking to protect themselves, seek also a reason why they cannot go. But I am ruthless. I insist.

Crossing the car park afterwards, I can see my mother's face set in a mask of hostility and hurt. She walks before me with short, angry strides.

I knew it would be this way. Standing earlier on stage at the back, behind the other peasants, or sitting quietly in the wings, I seem to hear the lines for the first time, every profanity, every curse, every sexual reference stabbing me as I know it stabs them out there in the darkness.

Afterwards, when the lights go up in the little local theatre where we are performing, I spy on them, hiding myself behind the others as we take a curtain call. She claps her hands stiffly as if they are deformed and will not bend, staring straight ahead, seeing nothing.

Now, sitting in the front seat of the car outlined by the headlights, I feel her searching for the words and phrases to give expression to her sense of the utter wrongness of what she had been forced to watch.

The words when they come are banal. Sitting, immobile, she says into the silent blackness, It isn't the sort of play a Christian should be in.

The banality of the words makes them harder to bear, makes them stay with me for many years. Their inadequacy and unsuitability express perfectly in their own way the hopelessness of the task of communicating to me her sorrow and her fear and her anger at my slipping away from all she had shaped me to be.

Later that evening when my father comes quietly to my bedroom to say goodnight, I am frightened to discover, lying like a weight inside me, a cold, wilful determination that things shall not rest.

I demand from him what he thought of the play. Oh good, my dear, very good, he says in a soothing, unhappy voice that is eager to please.

And then he, too, begins searching for words. He lowers his head as if in shame at some inadequacy in himself and I can feel him struggling for words. But . . . it's different you know . . . for us . . . he says, slowly and haltingly. The things they do in plays, you know . . . the things they say . . . they're not like us . . . you see . . . and his voice peters out humbly, so that he stands before me, silent, head bowed, asking for forgiveness.

Crushed by the stone of my anger which has toppled back upon me and feels now to be lying directly on my heart, I say nothing. I cannot speak and can only nod and smile unhappily.

Later, when he is gone, I weep, just like I am weeping now, at the memory of his shame, at the memory of the inarticulacy of our love, his and mine and hers, and at the memory, too, of a sharp, wicked little crack which I saw then appearing and which I know one day widened into a huge chasm, unbreachable by a kiss or an embrace or even by the last desperate grasp of repentant fingers.

*

It is about this time that John starts to come to tea. I have known John all my life – as a child since I grinned at him and tried to catch his eye as he pumped the old organ on a Sunday night.

For some time now John has called for me in his car to take me to the Youth Fellowship on Friday nights and brought me home from the Bible Study. But now he has taken to coming to tea on Sundays, occasionally with his mother, so that I think it is the case that plans, however vague and loose, are being laid for John and me.

At first when I think of it I am outraged. But then afterwards I soften. John is tall and blond, still too young and moon-faced to be handsome. His body is gangling and so too are his manners, and yet walking in beside him to the Bible Study or the Youth Fellowship pleases my vanity.

Snatches of conversation I have overheard make me believe the meeting thinks us a handsome couple so that sometimes this vague understanding between us makes me feel not outraged but rather comfortable, secure in the knowledge that something is planned.

John speaks at an open-air rally one Saturday afternoon in the shadow of the old stone cross in the market place.

Afraid of being recognized I stand at the edge of the little crowd from the meeting.

Our hymn drifts away among the sound of the car horns and the clicking heels of the shoppers. John reads from his Bible and then, a little red-faced at his own temerity, begins calling on the passers-by. Except a man be born again, he tells them, he cannot enter the Kingdom of Heaven. He shouts his message above the noise of the traffic and the music from a nearby record shop. The passers-by smile at him, those who know him, or at others they recognize in the group. Some take the tracts that are offered them, dropping them into deep shopping bags where they will lie undisturbed for many Saturdays. Others brush past the outstretched hands, or sidle or even contort their bodies to avoid them.

As the group sings another hymn I walk idly around the watchers with a collecting tin. A balding, middle-aged man standing on the outskirts of the crowd reaches into the pocket of his denim jacket as I approach.

He pulls out his hand as I reach him and peering into my face, extends it to push a grubby, brassy farthing through the slot in the top of the tin.

Together we watch as if in slow motion as the long, slim fingers press the little coin in and listen as it drops with a long, tinny tinkle on the empty bottom of the tin.

The man stares at me, defiant and derisory, a mocking, questioning smile playing upon his lips.

For a moment we stand together, united by the sight and the sound of the farthing. And then I smile at him, a rueful smile that turns into a grimace, and then I shrug. And then I walk away from him, the farthing clinking in the bottom of the tin, lonely and hollow and worthless.

*

Everything is slipping away from my mother and she knows it. When Jane invites me to stay for the weekend my mother insists that she receive a letter from Jane's mother, properly requesting my visit. I rage. I moan. I say, People don't do that these days. But my mother insists and there is dignity in her insistence.

Jane laughs easily and not unkindly when I tell her, red with embarrassment.

The next day she arrives at work with a piece of her parents' handsome headed notepaper. She types out a warm and polite invitation which she signs with her mother's name. She explains that her mother would do it herself but is rushing to finish a paper she has to give at a conference.

Later, I turn my head away in pain as my mother reads the letter carefully, her head moving from side to side a little as she follows the words, lingering, comforted, and even a little impressed over the italicized, black-lettered, 'Rev'.

She sits down at her little desk and opening it up, pulls forward a writing pad, tearing off a sheet of paper with great deliberation as if intent upon a serious and important task.

I want to take Jane's letter from her hand then, screw it into a tiny ball and hurl it to the far corner of the room.

Following her hand as she writes slowly and deliberately, occasionally lifting her head to stare at the wall as she contemplates a word, I want to drop on my knees before her. I want to take her by the shoulders and shake her, screaming the truth of the silly, harmless letter and her own absurd naïvety into her face.

And then I want to drop my head into her skirts and roll my face in them and feel, for one last time, the touch of confused, hesitant but loving fingers upon my head.

*

It is the books I first notice at Jane's. Books everywhere – reaching to the ceiling in shelves, turning up in odd places, at the top of the stairs in little over-stuffed bookcases, tumbling from between pots and jars in the kitchen, rising from the floor in stacks, even in the bathroom.

And the untidyness of everything, the pans and the chipped mugs and the packets in the kitchen, spilling out and not packed away like at home behind the cool frosted glass of the kitchen cabinet.

And the green everywhere, the plants hanging and trailing and twisting as if the huge, overgrown garden, unable any longer to contain itself, is now creeping in through the doors and the windows.

But perhaps what moves me most is the music, the music that fluted out of the half-open door in a stream of dancing, quivering notes as I entered, that paused and then gathered itself together into a slow, searching melody that snatched at me as I passed, telling me it had all my life in it, past and future, if I would but listen.

For sitting in Jane's father's study, contemplating this new and beautiful world through the rich, ruby red window of a raised wine glass later, it seems to me that all is music here.

Jane and her parents are talking about the play, using words and phrases meaningless to me. I close my eyes to take another deep, satisfying draught of the wine and as I do so their voices become distant and indistinct and melodic so that it seems to me that I am listening again to the fluttering notes I heard before slipping out through the unclosed door.

Suddenly there is a break in the melody. They have turned to me now and are asking me if my parents enjoyed the play. It is a pleasant and polite enquiry, made in their soft, melodic tones.

I am caught unprepared and I stammer an answer that is jagged and discordant after the grace and harmony of their conversation.

I say, It is not really their sort of play, and they look at me enquiringly and wait for me to tell them more.

So I try again. I say, My father thought it was well acted but . . . and there the sentence trails away again into the silence.

And then I hear a voice, cracked and ugly with unhappiness. My mother says it's not the sort of play a Christian should be in, it tells them.

Then it seems as if the spell has been broken. In place of the

83

ugly voice is one of great delicacy telling a story very softly, beautiful and sad.

Before me three heads nod in sympathy. I am telling them everything, about the fear and the loneliness, the shame and the embarrassment. I am telling them about Uncle Ezra and Aunt Esther, about my father and mother. I am telling them everything and yet something is missing so that the spectres of those I speak of rise up in the room in protest. They hover around my chair, nervous and betrayed in this new and beautiful world of books and music and soft, sophisticated words.

I long to stop the voice as it tells its story. I long to shout it down. I long to leap up and say, It isn't true. All this isn't true. At least not quite. I long to point at the spectres and say, Let them speak. But I cannot. I cannot stop the voice for the voice is mine.

At last all is quiet and then, into the silence washes a tide of gentle and understanding kindness.

I close my eyes to cut out their sympathy and to hide the sight of the ghosts, sad and distracted, slipping shamefaced, out through the door.

Something wet is splashing down on to my fingers squeezed tightly around the glass and into the rich, ruby red wine still waiting to be drunk.

*

They helped me to bed, Jane and her mother, up the wide, handsome staircase, to a bedroom of flowered curtains and bedspread with faded rugs and old-fashioned furniture painted white.

I fell asleep almost immediately, the sweet smell of old, fragrant bed linen in my nostrils, the lullaby of soft, earnest conversation in the room below in my ears.

*

I awoke to a tap on my door and Jane with a breakfast tray. She sat on the edge of the bed as I ate, looking deeply into my face and squeezing my hand. She poured my tea and fetched me oranges. All day it was like this, being petted as if I was sick or special.

Now I am sitting in the chair where last night I called up the phantoms, facing her father.

He is talking about a Crisis of Faith. How Jane had it, which is why she no longer goes to church, and how he sat her down in this chair and talked to her, just as he is talking now to me.

His round face beneath its thinning hair is warm with concern. His hands are clasped across his full belly as he puffs on his pipe, the smoke drifting and curling up above his head like a halo.

He is saying faith is a personal thing which is why Jane must be allowed to do what she wants to do. It is not something, he says, which can be forced. Questioning, he says, is not wrong. On the contrary, it can be the richest part of faith.

Jane's father is on his feet now, walking up and down, looking through the window and jabbing his pipe into the air as he talks of Life and Faith and Belief.

I watch him mesmerized, sleepy after the wine at lunch, full of food and fine feeling.

Suddenly, through the haze of contentment, I realize he is saying something shocking.

He is saying people must find their own God.

Naturally, Maud, he is saying, sitting himself down again and relighting his pipe, We don't expect anyone to believe any longer in a God with a long beard looking down on the world from a cloud. That sort of God is really no good to anyone, says Jane's father. Find your own God, Maud, he says, puffing contentedly at the ceiling.

I ponder what he said for the rest of the day.

Excused church to find our faith on our own, we let Jane's father go off to preach while we watch old films on the television.

I will not admit it to myself but I feel a little shocked at what he told me. The fact is I do think of God as bearded and angry and looking down from the heavens and worse, I've never had

85

the slightest difficulty believing in him this way. Furthermore it's not this image that seems foolish to me but any other one that anyone might try and put in its place.

Jane's father says that God is all around us and inside us. That God is part of what we are. But these words mean nothing to me.

All my life has been a battle with this tyrannous, inflexible, demanding presence, none the less real for being unseen. Now I scent victory and Jane's father cannot sweep away my triumph from me like this at a stroke.

*

I hide from my mother that I have not been to church. When she asks what Jane's father preached on, I say Life and Faith and Belief.

Looking at her, I cannot help but compare her with Jane's mother. Jane's mother looks bookish and always slightly untidy like the house. There is a softness about her and an ease with life that Jane has inherited.

Her smooth dark hair is always caught up in a crown on her head and pinned loosely, so that whisps fall down around her ears to be rescued and re-pinned as she talks.

Now, looking at my mother, I want to run my fingers through her dark, tightly permed curls, to ease them away from her head, to set them free.

I want to stand like this before her, my fingers in her hair, forehead to forehead, locked together, silent and still with the world whirling on past us.

For things are moving quickly now and I know, like her, that what we have and what we are is slipping away.

A change is coming over me, a change inside, as slow and deliberate and irreversible as the outward change that moved me on from girlhood to womanhood.

Inside me at my centre, something hard is growing. Around it my whole being is shuffling off something old and soft, preparing to emerge new and tight and brittle.

I am simmering with a sense of possibility, with an anticipation so real I could stretch out and grasp it. I think I am waiting for something. I think I am waiting for someone.

For life running on in leaps and bounds like this has carried me laughing and breathless up a high mountain. It has whispered softly and wickedly in my ear that everything before me can be mine and when I look down I see that everything is Frank.

For I am in love with Frank and tomorrow, after work, sitting in the corner of the settle in the bar I, Maud, who wooed Jane's parents with my melancholy tale of woe will woo Frank too.

I will see the glittering dark eyes soften, will feel a light and sympathetic touch from a black-bangled hand as I pour into his ear my love potion, the story of my life.

And when he drives me home later I shall feel the press of his lips on mine, the gentle caress from a crooked and caring finger down the side of my face so that later, at home, I shall be on fire and shall think that every inch of me burns and is alive and shall be, furthermore, astonished that anyone could be this happy.

Watch Maud give her heart then. Watch Maud throw open the door, not waiting for his knock, but tearing it open and throwing it back, calling out his name into the darkness, begging and imploring that he shall come to her.

For Maud thinks Frank will make her a new person. Maud thinks Frank will save her. Maud thinks Frank will bring her out of the dark and into the light. No wonder Maud wants to give her all to Frank.

*

John comes to tea almost every Sunday now. Sometimes even when I am not there. When I am at Jane's for instance. He sits at the table eating Sunday tea, the thin-cut white bread and coloured jelly, sits eating tea and talking to the preacher, without me. His blond head bows in grace beneath the plump and shining fruit on the Apples of Gold calendar with its wad of texts for each day, bows and lays claim to the place, where unlike me he looks right and proper and at home.

In the meeting now he sits in our row and afterwards folds his long, loping form on the seat beside me at the Bible Study where we chase old, obscure and lifeless texts from Deuteronomy and Ezekiel and Micah. One night a missionary comes instead to speak to us, casting lantern slides upon the pale blue wall, white smiles in dark faces, bright cotton frocks, low tin roofs in a hot, hot sun.

Next to me, in the half light of the noisy, buzzing old projector, John leans forward, his moon face bright with longing. On the way home he pulls the car off the road suddenly, almost in the spot where Frank parked the first night he kissed me.

He says, I must tell you, I've applied to Bible College. He says it with his hands still on the steering wheel, clenching it hard and staring straight ahead through the windscreen out into the night.

He says, I've been called. I know God's calling me.

Sitting next to him I feel the hairs stand up upon my scalp in loathing. An icy column of coldness rears up in my back. My hands clench in my lap in instinctive hatred and embarrassment at what he is saying.

And yet I feel sorry for him. Sorry that he chose to say this to me, this thing that means so much to him that means nothing to me.

I search for something to say, something to make him happy, and to camouflage my loathing.

Eventually, clearing my throat and shifting my legs I say, If it's what you want.

He turns his face to mine, shining and dedicated, his hands still clenched about the wheel as if in resolve. Oh no, he says, his voice dropping away in awe. It's what God wants.

*

I stay often now at Jane's. I do not tell my mother that we never go to church. Or that often Jane's mother and father are away so that the two of us are alone in the house to drink and hold parties as we wish. I do not tell her and she does not ask me. She does not ask me because she fears to know the answer. For my mother's mind has grown dark with fear, a new fear, beyond the reach of speech.

And she is right to feel afraid. For I am on a journey, I am on my way now, heading for those shuttered unspoken regions where her light is too faint and too embarrassed to shine.

I am heading there even now, this Saturday evening, sitting upon the manse steps, contemplating the wild, unruly beauty of the garden. It is late spring and all about me bursts with life. Bushes overhang the grass and trail their branches on the ground. Flowers bend beneath their own luscious richness. Even where I sit grass shoots up in the cracks between the paving stones, defying their weight and their greyness.

Music from the room behind me floods out through the french window, interwoven with the hubbub of voices the stamp of dancing and the clink of glasses.

Inside me my own bud of excitement is uncurling. For I have drunk more than usual and, as well, have taken several long gasping drags of a strange, sweet-smelling clumsy cigarette. At first I felt sick and my head spun which is why I came out to sit on the steps. But now with the rich sounds and sights around me it seems to me that I am thinking more deeply and clearly than usual, more deeply and clearly than I have ever thought in my life.

I am going over in my mind a scene which happened several minutes ago when I was in the lounge dancing, swaying against Frank, hands clasped and locked behind his neck, moving away only to take between my lips the end of the sweet-smelling cigarette. Stay with me, he said. Stay with me tonight.

Here, now, in the garden, the words hang in the night air, a question in the breeze, ruffling the heads of the flowers, demanding an answer in the rustle of the bushes.

Behind me there is a step. A hand, possessive and caressive, touches my back. A finger and a light black bangle stir the fine hairs upon my bare arms. I turn my face to the dark, darting eyes and the question there again before me, rippling in their depths.

Drawing away a little I touch, reverently, regretfully the skin

89

of his face, drawing it gently back with my fingers, marvelling all the while at its delicacy and paleness.

I reach to stroke the silky dark hair with fingers still light with wonder and as I do so feel again the sad, hopeless, dropping away in the pit of my stomach that I feel each time I stare at him so closely, so intimately like this.

He moves forward then to kiss me, his eyes bearing down on me, twin bullets. I start back from him and jump to my feet, rocking unsteadily with the movement.

With one sharp turn I am inside the french window and have closed it, turning the key.

For a moment he does not move, his back towards me. A slow, long spiral of smoke drifts up from his cigarette. Then it disappears before his face and having taken a drag he rises leisurely and easily to his feet.

He turns and looks at me across the stones. Taking one final drag of the cigarette, he flicks it carelessly away into the darkness and begins to walk towards me.

At the window his face rears up, the eyes glittering, the lips half-smiling, almost touching the glass.

Moving instinctively towards them, my fingers brush instead the coldness of the window. I spread them out across the thin transparent barrier – all that's left between the question and the answer.

And then I smile too and move my hand to turn the key. I open the door out towards him, listening all the time as he enters for what my voice will say.

All right, it says. All right.

*

Later, much later, lying beside his sleeping body, I wonder at the strangeness of it all, the fear and the disappointment and the all-pervading contentment of my own body, throbbing in newly discovered places, hollow and empty after so much effort.

I had lain beneath him tense and questioning. When he entered me I cried out, first with the surprise and then with the pain, so that he drew back sharply, uncertain and upset. But I held his head then fiercely in my hands, the black hair in my fingers and I begged him to go on.

I begged him to go on because I knew it must not stop. That this was the way it should be. I told him, Go on, Go on, and I thought, Everything must go on now. And then I closed my eyes with the hurt of it and clamped my teeth tightly together so I should not cry out again, murmuring inexpert endearments as he drove his body into mine, feeling an absurd new pleasure in my own pain.

He came to rest finally stretched upon me, his head inert against my shoulder and later slipped away from me unspeaking with a kiss rehearsed and thoughtful but still perfunctory.

He lies beside me now, a body sleeping, a light and even breath in the silence.

Reaching down I feel the sticky dampness beneath my legs. Easing myself slowly off the mattress, I get to my feet, a little shaky and uncertain, and pad, silent and naked to the door.

Feeling for the knob I let myself out, the door clicking softly. I feel my way along the corridor, the carpet thin and threadbare beneath my shoeless feet.

Reaching the bathroom I switch on the light and close the door behind me, shooting the bolt.

Then, alone, in the harsh glare of the unshaded bulb I examine the redness of my thighs. Long smudges of blood are drying on the skin and as I stand, awestruck and a little proud, a last delicate rivulet of red trickles out before me.

Quietly and cautiously I run some water into the bath. When it has reached several inches deep I lower myself into, sinking into it as far as I can go and letting it wash over me. I lay there for a few minutes overcome with a feeling of tiredness. Then, feeling chilled, I sit up and slowly begin to soap away the blood, watching it slip away in the water and disappear.

Returning to the bedroom and opening the door, I seem to see the scene before me like a painting, a still-life purposefully assembled to be remembered many years on.

My clothes lie with Frank's over the old fireside chair by the round-topped gas fire. Beside it on the hearth are the two tumblers with rings of red in the bottom and the wine bottle, all but empty, and leaning against it with an air of neglect, a guitar, one string broken and shooting out in an arc from the neck.

In the bed his back gleams a silvery white in the early morning light, his hair black against the pale pillow.

The soft, careless breathing makes me feel cold and lonely so that I reach to the chair for the cardigan and walk to the window. There I put the cardigan around my shoulders and perch myself upon the arm of a dusty old sofa to watch the dawn.

Already, outside the window, the darkness is turning to an icy, crystal, perfect blue. It lights up the grey, dewy slates on the roofs beneath the attic window and then, as I continue to watch as at some show or performance, turns itself golden and honey-coloured and begins to pour upon the houses, the tree tops, the fields and the hills and over my arms and neck and face as I stare entranced from the sofa.

It is then, warm from the first rays of the sun and feeling, at last, a little sleepy, that I remember the prophecy, the words they have read to me, and preached to me and prayed to me for so long.

And opening my eyes to see the glorious, golden world before me, I finally believe them to be true.

For looking out over the town to the hills and finally to the sky, it seems to me I truly see a new heaven and a new earth. And further, reaching down to touch my own curious, contented tenderness, it seems to me to be true that an old heaven and an old earth have during the night quite passed away.

And then, as if to tell me that what has passed away is gone for ever and can never be recovered there is a movement from the bed. Turning, I find myself looking again into the dark eyes. Without removing my gaze from his face, I cross back across the floor. I drop my cardigan on to the chair and lower myself to the mattress, slipping smoothly and silently beneath the covers to bury my face in modest delight in his throat.

I feel his arms envelop me then, his lips at my ear. Happy Birthday, he says, to my hair, a laugh in his voice. I raise my head and look again in his eyes. In them I see the reflection of the window and of the dawn beyond. It is light. The night is past. It is a new day. And today I am seventeen.

*

I had an argument with John once, coming home from the Bible Study. It was one Sunday night not long after I'd seen Frank for the first time at the evangelist's rally. At the Bible Study group we'd been discussing the Song of Solomon. The leader said it was a book of prophecy. He read out part of it in a low, precise voice. He read, He brought me into the banqueting house and his banner over me was love.

He read it as if the words were dusty and he finished it with a dry little cough and then said it was his favourite text, a beautiful text, a gospel text, foretelling Jesus Christ.

In the car I said, It's rubbish, It's not true. I said it passionately, glowering at the road before me so that I saw John's head move in nervous, sidelong glances.

I said, It's a love song, Anyone can see it's a love song. Don't you see it's a love song, I said, turning to him, clenching my fists before him. But he wouldn't look at me. He just stared straight ahead but I noticed the cheek turned towards me had turned red with embarrassment.

He cleared his throat a couple of times and I thought he would speak but nothing came out. I realized then that I'd shocked him. That he thought he'd heard something he shouldn't from someone he hadn't expected to hear it from. I saw he was frightened. But I didn't feel sorry for him. I was angry.

I turned away from him to the window. There was silence and then I said it one more time, the thing that had hurt him and made him feel nervous and then finally afraid. I said, It's a love song.

*

It won't leave me all day, that feeling that the new heaven and the new earth have arrived, not even after we have faced each other across the pillow, finally embarrassed in the light of late

93

morning, of the real day, not even after we have dressed, together, politely averting our eyes. It will not leave me even after the crystal early-morning blue that turned to honey gold has dulled finally to grey. And so I carry it home with me, in my arms, glowing with the wonder of it still. I carry it right home, in through the back door, to the kitchen where I stop with it, sharply, before my mother, seated on the old, low chair by the stove, a look of the most dreadful suffering upon her face.

The story inches out then between her tight, strained lips while my father shuffles papers unseeingly at his desk, his head lowered, the back that faces us tense with listening.

Sitting propped up in bed that morning, chewing leisurely upon their toast and marmalade before leaving for the Sunday morning meeting, they had idly switched on the radio and so had heard the voice of Jane's father. He was talking about the problem of belief. He told my parents what he had told the people at the conference where he had been speaking, what he told me that day in his study. He told them no one could believe any longer in a God with a long beard looking down from a cloud, an angry God, a vengeful God. He said no one knew what God was. He was all round us, inside us, part of what we were.

He wasn't the Old Man in the Sky, he said, a half-chuckle hiding in his soft academic voice.

That was the worse part for them, the Old Man in the Sky. My mother switched off the radio then with a snap. She had heard enough. She threw back the blankets and reached for her dressing gown.

Like me my parents had no difficulty in believing in the Old Man in the Sky, that was what God was for them. They knew the Devil was abroad in the world, set upon undermining the Word. The Devil had a silver tongue and offered gods other than the real God, whose worship led only to damnation. They thought Jane's father, if not the Devil himself, was almost certainly one of his disciples.

Thus my mother walked firmly to the phone to call me at Jane's and tell me to come home, immediately. Only I wasn't there and Jane's little brother, displeased at being roused from bed so early on a layabed Sunday, told her so.

It must have seemed to her in that moment that all her worst fears for me were realized, all the fears she could not speak, rushing up in a flood and swirling in a wordless chaos in her mind. This is how it is still as she sits now before me, angry and fearful but most of all distressed.

I meanwhile am cold and calm and unafraid. There is no chaos in my mind, merely clear, sharp purpose. The knot of hardness has been untying itself inside me and uncoiled now lies like steel, ramrod straight.

I stare into her eyes refusing to be caught, or shamed or abashed, refusing to be drawn into her web of embarrassment and sorrow.

I wasn't at Jane's, I say, my eyes never leaving hers, but boring down into them, piercing further with every word. I was at Frank's.

I was at Frank's, I say, My boyfriend, Frank.

And then I lie. I lie so well, so convincingly I almost believe it myself, this story, this fiction that pretends that what took place never happened.

I say, I went with Frank to his flat because the party was so noisy and I don't care for loud music. We sat up talking late into the night, he and I and the people he lives with. It was very late when I realized the time, too late to go back to Jane's. There was a spare room, for someone was away and I slept there.

I say, It was silly to sit up late because now I'm tired, and I yawn, calmly and easily, and I smile.

She blinks at me then, confused, wondering at her own next move, wanting it to be the truth, everything she has heard, wanting to know but not to know. Her lips make a small movement in response to my smile. I see her relaxing, slightly, wanting to smile like me. I have her now and I move in for the kill.

I let the smile that had warmed my face begin to fade slowly. I let anger rise in my eyes.

What did you think had happened? I say, my face innocent and merciless.

She blushes then, my mother, a deep ugly red that shows up the tiny veins in her face, a red that reaches right up to her dark, tight curls. She drops her eyes at the look of incredulous horror that now I have allowed to flood across my face.

What did you think had happened, I hiss, lingering over the words, stretching them as upon a rack.

My mother sits, motionless and humiliated, struck dumb by her inability to voice the fears and horrors so real and painful yet so hopelessly without name or even shape.

We didn't know, she says eventually, pitifully, almost whimpering and glancing all the while at my father's face as it bows, alert and tense, over its papers.

Aware perhaps at how far it has all slipped away from her, she seems to gather herself together, giving herself a small shake.

This young man, she says, taking courage with each word, seeing suddenly again a rightness that had for a moment been lost.

This young man. We don't know him. You never brought him here.

Her head now is raised. Her eyes are beginning to challenge mine again. The flush is disappearing.

You never brought him here. You must bring him. We must meet him. He must be brought into the meeting.

Her head is up now, square with mine. Her eyes clear and forceful. She repeats, He must be brought into the meeting, tapping the wooden arm of the chair with knuckles white with effort, clenched in readiness for disagreement.

And that is when it ends, with me, staring at the knuckles white and waiting for another round. And after this one another and another. No. No more. This is when it ends, when I finally bring her house of sin and salvation, heaven and hell tumbling around her like a pack of cards.

For the briefest of moments I stand before her, Samson with the pillars of Armageddon in his hands, waiting, wondering whether to do it. But already the steel has risen inside me for one last effort. Yes, it says, Yes, and I feel the pillars crack and strain, the roof shudder, the building topple and lurch and then the whole earth tremble as it crashes down around the three of us.

Bring him into the meeting, I say, Why should I do that? I don't even know if I believe myself.

For a moment there is silence, the silence of those who stand stock still in the surrounding rubble, shocked to find themselves still alive.

And then I make a sudden, sharp movement, consumed with a passionate desire to be away from her, to be away from them both.

I dart to the stairs and hurl myself up them two at a time almost tearing the old banister from its roots. Pausing at the top for an instant I turn. It is only for a second and yet it is long enough for what is before me to imprint itself upon my memory for ever.

By the stove still sits my mother, her face raised towards me, a picture of confusion and suffering, the first tears beginning to slip down her cheeks.

At the foot of the stairs stands my father who has turned from the desk and whose face is now upraised too towards mine, shocked and sad, but most of all pleading.

And in the middle of the tragedy, a comic touch, John, peering around the back door like an actor in the wrong play, his pleasant face bemused, embarrassed but still unashamedly curious.

*

Who knows what exactly happens that night?

In my bedroom all the cold courage and the steel collapses and I begin to weep too. I weep for hours, on and on, till I have a headache that thumps and thunders and pushes everything but pain from my mind.

I do not hear my father when he knocks upon the bedroom door. I only know he is beside me when I feel his calloused workman's hands gently stroking my forehead, trying to stroke away the pain and trying in the simple, loving gesture to beg for time and for understanding in the face of all our inabilities to find a solution.

On and on he strokes. Once he says in a voice unaccusing and sad, Your mother's downstairs weeping.

I say, And I'm up here weeping, and I turn my head in an angry thrust to one side of the pillow that makes the pain stab afresh.

I think he understands. I feel but do not see him nod at the futility of it all.

Later he goes away and when he returns he says, May John come and see you? I shout then, No, No, Oh God, No, in outrage, in revulsion, thrashing my head from side to side so that he begins shushing me, like a child.

Through the pain I can hear the murmur of prayers. I think they pray long into the night, for, slipping in and out of sleep, I believe I still hear them. I think the voices grow louder, as if more people have joined. I think I hear Uncle Ezra's voice, raised above the rest, loud and distinct, calling on the Lord for Maud's soul.

I want to stop up my ears, I want to scream at them to be quiet. I turn my face to my father and tell him fiercely to stop them but it comes out as a whisper and it seems my father does not hear, for he just goes on, stroking, stroking.

Then, just when I think I can hear singing, the voices fade away, deeper and deeper into the distance and I fall deeply and fully into sleep. For I am tired with the pain and the weeping, tired too of the fighting, but most of all tired because I was up early this morning, up early at the window in the attic room, up early to welcome in the new heaven and the new earth.

*

Bring him into the meeting, I said. Why should I do that? I don't even know if I believe myself.

Written down now, black and white, the words are simple, even pathetic. And yet, twenty years on I am still amazed that I said what I said.

Coming down to breakfast the morning after it seems to me

98

that even the very walls of the house stand shocked and silent at the awfulness of what was spoken.

On the staircase an embroidered text, 'Remember thy Creator in the days of thy Youth', worked by my mother in the sanatorium as a child, hangs crooked, dashed out of place the night before as I fled up the stairs. There is something utterly improper about it hanging aslant still, about it not having been gently touched back into position. It hangs a little crazily on the wall of the house like a slipped strap on a distraught, normally prim and immaculate old lady, the first small warning that things ahead might not be what they had always been.

I see I have won the day, if winning was what I wanted.

My mother serves me breakfast as if I were a guest, silent and heavy, laying before me, beside the food, birthday presents, forgotten yesterday, today awkward and out of place. Beneath the paper a new copy of the Sunday morning hymn book, gold lettering on red with a black silk marker, accuses me.

Standing at the stove as I open my parcel, my mother's eyes are downcast but still defiant. Without looking at me she says, You may change it, if it's not what you want. In the Bible shop, I ask myself, for what? I lay the hymn book aside to eat.

My father too rustles deferentially around me in the kitchen, casting furtive almost timid glances at me as he pretends to go about his business.

There is no pleasure in my victory. I am sad at the sight of his deference, of her subservient defiance.

Later I try to explain it all to Frank, the pain and the triumph and the emptiness.

I find him curiously distant. No, not distant, but not close like I had thought he would be close, close as I had thought I had a right to expect him to be close with all that had happened.

I wanted . . . what did I want? His sympathy? His sympathy, yes of course, but his admiration too. I wanted him to say, Well done. And I wanted his wisdom. I wanted him to be wiser than me and I thought he would be because I thought that was the way it worked, the way it was. I wanted him to say, Yes I see, this is the way it happened and this is what it all means and this is what you should do.

But instead, sitting opposite him in the bar after work, I find only this – distance, and in his eyes a curious vacancy with, behind it, what may be the first flutterings of faint alarm.

I want to tell him then not to be frightened. I want to lay my hand upon his arm and say, Don't worry. But I can't. For I am in love with Frank and it's too late for I am frightened myself. Already some part of me knows that things are not going right, that it should all have been easier than this. Some part of me realizes already that falling in love needs to take its own time, that it must not have at its back this urgency, pushing it forward, taking its breath away, making it scrabble around like this for signs of love and consolation.

At the bar, buying another drink, I see his fine, handsome face reflected way back behind the line of bottles and I see it looks disturbed. I see his long delicate fingers rolling a cigarette with tense, hurried movements.

Later, entering his room for the second time to make love, it seems everything before me is the same, but different, as if the room had been painted again by a second painter with a different perspective and a different palette.

It is still not dark and the summer evening light strains insistent and mocking through the thin curtains, demanding our embarrassment at the earliness of the hour.

Facing each other, interlocking as if according to a plan, we discover, too late, we are insufficiently drunk so that our love-making, still new and unsure is forced and quick, refusing all our efforts to draw it out or make it easy.

Beside me, afterwards, Frank's eyes are closed but I know he does not sleep. I look at his face hard and think I see dissatisfaction and irritation lurking in the creases of his eyes, in the corners of his lips.

I want to reach out to stroke the smoothness of his skin for, if anything, the touching of his body, of his realness, gives me the most pleasure. But something prevents me, an unsureness that it is permitted, a lack of knowledge of the rules of the game.

When I get home Uncle Ezra is waiting. I suspect him of being there for several hours. I suspect him of praying for me.

We sit opposite each other, alone, Uncle Ezra and I, in the gathering gloom in the unused, inhospitable front room. I sit, almost at his feet, in the low sofa. He looks down, the inquisitor, from the high-backed chair.

I see but do not hear his lips framing words, questions, framing sympathy, advice, threats and promises.

Uncle Ezra is telling me I will be lost. Uncle Ezra is telling me I will be left behind. Uncle Ezra is speaking of the Lake of Fire, of the Bottomless Pit. But all these things I know and Uncle Ezra does not frighten me.

Only one thing frightens me, one thing that drives all other thoughts from my mind, one thing that so preoccupies my thoughts that this man before me seems a stranger and his words a foreign language. The thing that frightens me is that Frank does not love me.

Only a little while, Maud, says Uncle Ezra, leaning forward in the chair.

Excuse me, I say, politely with a smile, getting up from the sofa as if I had not heard him, making my name die on his lips with astonishment.

I'm tired, I say, as if the interview is over, instead of just beginning. I must go to bed, I say, with another vague and kindly smile.

I thought when I fell in love with Frank that he would love me. I thought that was the way it would fall, the pattern of events, like the way the shaken glass falls, neatly and prettily in the kaleidoscope.

Closing the door on Uncle Ezra's shocked face I feel fear and panic rising inside me. It makes me want to choke. But it makes me want to laugh too, wild, hysterical laughter.

I think Frank does not love me and I think he never will. I think he will soon leave me. Only a little while, Maud, I scream at myself silently as I walk up the stairs. Only a little while.

*

101

And it is.

Within a month Frank is gone from the factory.

Afterwards they call it The Incident at Section Four. That's how they speak of it too, years afterwards, Frank's contemporaries, dividing diametrically into two opposing camps, those who speak his name with pride, as of a folk hero; those who grimace and say they always knew he wouldn't be the man his father was.

Poor Frank. How could he be the man his father was? How could he be a raggedy child missing school to dig peat on the moors to carry it round the houses in a hand-cart?

How could he be the man who sold the peat and saved and one day bought the land and worked and worked and one day sold the land and bought a factory?

The neat signature that appears on the company memoranda and letters is not Frank's father's although it says it is, but his secretary's, a woman who keeps the secret that everybody knows, that Frank's father scratches out his own name with only the greatest difficulty and concentration.

Unable, virtually, to read or write, he sends Frank, the only son Frank, to the best schools and to the best university.

And now, agonizing honestly over the impossible task of replacing somehow the spirit of endeavour of the peat bogs in his beloved son's well-favoured life, he hits upon the idea of sending him to the factory floor.

Poor Frank, he hates it on the line. He wants to like it, life among the common man and woman on the jolting, juddering assembly line. But he hates it.

He wants to be happy, immersed in the bawdy, small-town camaraderie. But he isn't.

In fact, it bores him and he despises it which makes him, in turn, despise himself.

For Frank is young and wishing to be Everyman. He wants his education not to matter, not to set him above the crowd, but it won't be cast aside like that and pokes its head through the fog of idle, vulgar chit-chat that surrounds Frank on the line, winking at him and raising its eyebrow.

Poor Frank. He wants to please his father, this bluff, red-faced man he loves whose fleshy hand is too big and awkward to grasp a pen and prefers to clap itself in open admiration around the shoulders of his son.

Poor Frank. He wants to please his father. But how can he go back to the peat bogs?

*

Frank has been two weeks on the line, growing gloomier and grimmer. He turns round to us occasionally as we watch him, Jane and I, from our glass cage, grinning at us a wry and shaky grin. Sometimes he slides from his stool with a nod at Jane who slips from her desk with a cigarette which she passes to him in a tiny cupboard-liked office out of sight of the line.

Twice a day his irritation and dissatisfaction congeals into a melting, white hot fury.

Twice a day, mid-morning and mid-afternoon, the shuddering buzz of the conveyor belt is drowned for half an hour by music.

It booms out, gay and gaudy through the speaker high up on the factory floor wall which otherwise orders people to their offices or to take telephone calls.

The music, broadcast over the Tannoy, comes from a radio in the telephonist's tall little cubicle in the factory entrance hall.

In charge of the radio is the telephonist, a bird-like woman with pinned-up bouffant hair who, when she answers the phone, speaks the name of the company in a high artificial voice that seems to slide down the inside of her nose into the receiver slung beneath her bright red lips.

Every time, without fail, she turns on the radio too early, in the middle of the news bulletin that precedes the music. Every time without fail her blood red-tipped fingers fly to the knob to turn down the sound as if in the news we should all hear something we should not.

Up and down goes the sound as she tries to catch the moment when the signature tune of the music programme starts. Tantalizing words and phrases from the news bulletin spew out

103

as she turns the knob and we strain to reassemble the jigsaw puzzle of sound.

Her orgy of knob-twiddling annoys us all it reduces Frank to a simmering fury. Several times he has tried to interest his father in the problem. But Frank's father is preoccupied of late. He has spent many hours closeted alone with the company accountant and now has more to think about than the irritating ways of the telephonist.

On the afternoon the incident occurs, the announcer's voice booms in and out of the silence as usual. This time it hurtles out at us staccato bursts about a plane crash, a government scandal and the total of new American dead on an old Asian hillside.

Afterwards those near Frank said it was the last that did it. That before the news of the war he had just been seen to drum his fingers on the bench as he strained to hear, or stretch his legs fretfully from the stool.

But when the announcer began to speak in hiccuping bursts of the dead and the dying he swore softly under his breath and then out loud as he leaned forward.

It was when the war died away finally to return as the weather forecast that they said he rose to his feet and let out the bellow of dreadful desperation that raised every head on the factory floor including Jane's and mine bent over our desks.

Looking up through the glass I see him pick up the nearest object to his hand which happens to be a clip-board fluttering with overtime sheets.

Letting out another howl he raises it and in one smooth, furious movement hurls it, with all his strength, at the speaker.

Followed along its flight path by every eye, it smacks hard against the speaker fabric and falls with a clatter to the ground, scattering its sheets as it falls.

The announcer is forecasting showers as Frank turns again to the bench and reaches for a handful of components which in a second too are flying through the air and spilling down the front of the speaker.

For a moment the line seems frozen, all eyes upon the last of the components still rolling merrily and eccentrically around the floor.

Then, just as the first stirring notes of the signature tune breaks out over them as if this indeed was the sign, the line leaps into life. Half-made products, biros, hand tools, wire baskets of documents, chalk, pencils, a shoe and a plastic mug rain down upon the speaker from all sides.

Watching the avalanche nervously from the safety of the office I feel a movement beside me and Jane is gone, to stand before the speaker as if before a god and then to aim at it a heavy stapler and a file of letters.

A metal stool from the excitable Pole who had sworn at me on my first day at work finally brings the speaker crashing from the wall. It smashes upon the ground to the shouts and cheers of those watching, its wires trailing like entrails.

When the personnel manager and the foreman arrive Section Four is a litter of ruined products and shop floor bric-à-brac. The conveyor belt is at a standstill and there is a festival air about the place. Workers have left their seats to talk to friends further down the line and now sit beside them, chatting idly and smoking forbidden cigarettes.

Jane and Frank meanwhile are in the tiny cupboard-like office where Frank goes for his forbidden smokes. They are howling and clasping themselves with wild, uncontrolled laughter watched by me, leaning with my back against the locked door.

Tears run down Jane's face, tears which she wipes delicately away with one finger around the coal black line of her eye make-up. Her long earrings sway and dance with her laughter as if even they are enjoying the joke.

Frank rests against the wall, limp with the ecstasy of it, his head thrown back, one hand in his hair. His laughter fills the small room, raucous and wheezing, choked with its own physical effort.

As their howls begin to lessen, Frank reaches into his pocket and pulls out a crumpled pack of cigarettes. He offers it to Jane who takes one out, delicately, with two long fingers.

Together they put their cigarettes to their lips but then, as

Frank strikes a match, they begin to laugh again so that the match burns down and Frank has to drop it with a cry so that the howls start up again.

I watch them all the while as if they were strangers, or as if they were actors in a film playing before me.

The sound of their laughter echoes around my brain. It leaves them in huge waves which crash against corners of the tiny room.

My lips seem to be suspended on thin wires which move them in and out and up and down in a delicate dance, miming the first nervous, uneasy movements of a smile.

I want to laugh with them. I want so much to laugh with them, just like I wanted to laugh that day, all those years ago, with Matthew and Mikey and Corrie, that day my mother covered everything with her dull, grey cloud.

But my lips will only hover like this on the edge of a smile, and no matter how hard I try, no laugh will rise up inside me and spill out like theirs.

Watching them, Frank and Jane, I think they laugh like gods. Yes, like gods, chosen and golden, laughing together, their private joke, the secret of life, the secret they have grown up with and have known all their lives, that life is easy and absurd and the complications and the seriousness belong to other people.

Watching them I do not feel like laughing.

*

Frank tells his father he doesn't want to work in his factory any more.

Frank's father tells Frank it doesn't matter because soon the factory won't be his anyway.

Soon the factory will be taken over. Soon it will be full of fresh-faced, eager young men in smart dark suits and Frank's father will move out of his office to a smaller one at the end of the corridor. There he will be left to sign expenses chits and memos about the staff newsletter which nobody reads and everybody knows are signed by his secretary.

106

And some people will mutter about the changes and shake their heads and others who have cousins and uncles and brothers in other factories, and who want better money and the union like them, instead of the Summer Ball and the Christmas Party, will say, About time.

And so, it is the last Summer Ball we go to, Jane and Frank and I, along with the rest.

Frank has decided to use some money from a trust fund to travel overland to India to visit an ashram.

Actually, he says, I'm interested in religion.

I know, I say.

Jane is off, too, hitch-hiking to Greece before going to university in the autumn.

Actually, she says, I'll probably meet up with Frank somewhere on the way.

Quite likely, I say.

Now, dancing with me chastely and a little stiffly, Frank says, It's been fun, and smiles at me his warm, new, elder brother smile that softens his glittering dark eyes.

Sliding awkwardly around the dance floor of the local hotel like this, held woodenly like a puppet by this man who knows my dark and secret places, I am enraged.

I want to scream at him, It wasn't fun.

I want to scream at him, It wasn't fun and it isn't fair.

I want to say to him, Don't you see. I could have been like Jane if it all had been different.

I want to say to him, Give me time and I'll learn to be easy. Give me time and I'll laugh.

And I want to say to him, poor Frank, innocent Frank, for whom just by chance so much was lost and so much gained, I want to say to him, I want to say to him, because I am unhappy, Don't you know what I gave up for you?

For dancing here, stiff with misery and pain, I feel myself to be adrift for ever from the old world but alone too and ill at ease in the new one, that new one I welcomed in with such gladness in his room that morning.

Passing a long, gilt-edged mirror, I see myself reflected – a column of blackness in the dress my mother sewed with so much sorrow for the occasion.

Staring at my reflection, I catch his eyes in the mirror. You look beautiful, he says, gently, regretfully, as if by way of consolation.

Averting my eyes abruptly from his, I look again deep into my own pupils and see them shadow and darken till they seem to me to be as black as my dress.

Yes, I say, to my own reflection and then, Yes, again, turning my eyes away once more from my own to his.

Yes, I say finally, drawing away from him a little, to stare full in his face, to cast upon him a smile from cold, unfriendly lips, to look at him through eyes opaque with unflinching and unforgiving anger.

5

That dress, that sad, black satin dress. It is the last thing she sews. Afterwards it seems to me that she grew sick as she sewed it, so that I shiver sometimes and wonder if it was something she caught off its rustling, shiny blackness.

I know my mother is very sick, but I do not think she will die, until one day when I see him helping her slowly, painfully from her chair.

She grasps his arm as she struggles to her feet and then, standing, swaying upon thin, uncertain legs, she throws back her head suddenly and howls like an animal.

The noise rattles around the house, defying the embroidered reassurances on the walls and the pencilled messages of hope and certainty in the Bibles. It shakes the house to its very foundations with its anguish, its fear and its angry impotence.

Seeing it, and hearing it from the top of the stairs, I dart back out of sight to stand shaking against the corridor wall.

For some weeks now my parents have not been going to the Hall on Sunday's. Instead they have been going to the Baptist Chapel further down the road.

Sitting down to eat one night after the outburst I thought had ended it all, I saw my father shuffling his knife and fork and saw he had something to say.

He cleared his throat and, staring at his plate as if the words he needed were written there, said he and my mother would leave the Brethren if only I would go with them to another church.

Wrapped up in Frank and angry with them, too, for confusing my clean break with their compromise, I agreed.

I told them, carelessly, to choose a church themselves and they did, gathering newsletters and parish magazines and pouring over them like newly-weds looking for a house.

They picked the Baptist Chapel not far from the Hall and for several Sundays I went with them, bellicose and mutinous, despising the black-gowned minister and the coffee-morning friendliness.

Then one Sunday morning I simply stayed in bed. I settled back against the pillows with a book and when my mother looked into my room told her, without lifting my eyes, that I would not be going. I looked up only when I heard the defeated click of the bedroom door closing.

And so they went on their own to the Baptist Church – stranded there, not really at home but staying in the hope that one Sunday I would join them.

But I never did and now, hearing that dreadful cry I am frightened at what I have done.

For it seems to me that in tearing myself free I have torn up their faith too, that transplanted by its very roots by my rebellion, their faith has begun, almost imperceptibly but irreversibly to wither.

I know now that my mother soon will die and that while she may die with the old familiar phrases upon her lips, these phrases now do not bring the comfort they should, the comfort to which she is entitled, the comfort for which the whole of her life has been a down payment.

On the last night, she wakes for a moment from the fitful, fevered sleep that morphine brings and seems to me, sitting alone by the side of the iron cot, to be almost herself again.

She speaks my name quietly with a smile on her lips. Maud, she says, and then again, Maud, but more urgently this time, grasping my hand with her thin fingers.

One final time she tries again, Maud, she cries, staring at me with eyes full of desperation and yearning.

For a moment we look at each other, our eyes locked, she struggling for words, for an idea; me, gripping her fingers, willing her to speak. But then the sickness and the drugs overtake her again and her eyes begin to close. She sinks back muttering my name once before she is silent.

Half an hour or so later I am joined at the bedside by the wife of an elder from the meeting.

110

She bends over and taking my mother's hand gently from mine, strokes her hair and peers into her face. After a moment she lowers the hand respectfully and turns to me saying in a hushed, matter-of-fact voice, Her soul has departed.

It's all right now, she says, with a warm, quick smile. Her soul is with Jesus.

I look at her this woman with the lines across her forehead and her hair pulled into a bun and I know she tries to bring me consolation. She wants to console me for the sound of my mother's breath rattling out harsh and inhuman from between dry, fetid lips. Her words are words of kindness but to me they are obscenities.

She wants me to be glad that this shape, rattling and rumbling away before me, is just a shell and not my mother at all. She wants me to be glad that that which is truly my mother is away now, beside the throne in Paradise.

But I want to shout at her, this woman, that I don't care about her soul. I want to howl at her, What use is her soul?

I want to scream at her, I can't talk to a soul. It's her body I need, all of her together back here.

And then I want to sweep up my mother's thin and raddled form from the bed and hold it in my arms and hug it and kiss it, kiss the empty eyes and whisper to the deaf ears, Don't go. Come back. I have so much to tell you.

I want to whisper, I have so much to talk to you about. I have so much to explain.

I want to whisper, Don't go. I love you.

*

Which is why, you see, I hate Uncle Ezra when he grasps my hand by the graveside and tries to comfort me with his Only a little while, Maud.

I hate him because he can say this thing and believe it.

I hate him because for him there is no finality in the pale oak coffin, or the brass plate that spells her name or the handful of cold, wet earth flung in on top of it.

I hate him because I know that nothing in my life will ever be as final as the sight of that dark, ugly hole in the ground and the knowledge that in it, behind the hard polished wood, lies her body.

What would I give now to believe this is not the end? What would I give now to be able to build back up that temple of hopes and dreams of life beyond the grave that I so recklessly tore down? I would give everything. Of course, I would give everything.

Yes, Maud would repent now if she could. Maud would open the door. Maud would let Him into her heart. Maud would walk to the front. Maud would give them back her soul for one moment with the saints in glory, one moment to sit next to her mother and whisper in her ear, I'm sorry.

Yes, I would repent now. But it's too late. Just like they said it would be. Don't leave this Hall, don't leave this tent, or it'll be too late they said. And they were right.

I can't repent because I can't believe, and I can't believe because I've torn it all down and thrown it all away. And it can't be gathered together again.

And now all I can do is hate Uncle Ezra. Curse him, his heart, his life, his very being as he grasps my hand this way. Curse Uncle Ezra who listens for the sound of the trumpets every day and casts an eye at the heavens wondering if today's the day we shall all be together.

Curse you, Uncle Ezra, grasping my hand this way. Curse your sturdiness and confidence. Curse you for telling me, Only a little while. Curse me for knowing it's for ever.

*

Uncle Ezra was saved in the trenches, my mother in the sanatorium. But my father, he was led to Jesus in the High Street, one unseasonally warm October afternoon, by a girl with long legs in a slim-fitting suit, a pert hat upon her bush of brown hair and shy, owlish beauty escaping from behind her spectacles.

She put a tract into his hand and smiled and he fell in love and read it. Or may be it was the other way around.

Either way he went to the meeting, just like the tract invited him to do and he heard the message and believed. And he saw her again. Or maybe it was the other way around.

I have a picture of him now, taken on the day they got engaged, absurdly young in a new, unyielding uniform, a smile upon his face, both contented and bemused, as if he was, at the very moment the camera caught him, trying to figure out how life had moved so quickly. Well, it does, doesn't it, when you're in love?

Everything came together for my father. The son of a selfish, self-educated, self-opinionated father, determined to empty God of all its meaning for his sons, he was looking for love and faith when the tract was placed daintily upon his palm. So by a miracle he found the two together.

Looking back, I see they stayed that way for him, his love and faith permanently entwined. He lost heart and his faith when she died.

He stayed at the Baptist Church though, I think because it was easier to be anonymous among the hundred or so people who filled the pews there than among the sparse thirty or so dotted around the chairs of the Hall.

He went there, morning and evening, but more to fill up the hours I think than anything else.

In between he'd sit for long hours in the old rocking chair, his head back, his eyes closed, moving it gently and very quietly backwards and forwards.

One Sunday we were together after lunch, he in the chair, me at my mother's bureau writing a letter, when suddenly he broke the silence.

We just did what we thought was right, Maud, he said, not opening his eyes, his voice full of suffering.

I know, I know, I said.

We wanted what was best for you. We prayed about it all the time.

I know, I said, I know.

We thought you'd want what we wanted.

You weren't to know, I said.

*

113

The card says Uncle Ezra's been called home. It says he kept the faith and I believe it.

Over the years, wherever I went, the texts and the calendars followed me, even when I went half way across the world, in that place where I paused, one early morning, to think of Matthew.

On my birthday and at Christmas would come sweet-smelling soaps or delicately embroidered handkerchiefs from Aunt Esther and, from Uncle Ezra, a calendar with texts for every day that I would never hang on the wall or a bookmark bright and golden with scripture for a Bible which I no longer opened.

Sometimes, when I tore off the wrapping paper, I laughed and sometimes I mocked, tossing the calendar across the table to a lover.

Sometimes I let the bookmark with its text tell my old tale of woe for me, let it win for me a soft, gentle squeeze of my hand across the discarded paper and string. And sometimes I was angry, tearing it sharply in many pieces and throwing it in the waste bin as I had done with the other one so many years earlier.

But Uncle Ezra never gave up. A few months ago, old and very frail, he propped himself up in bed on stick-like arms to reach for his directory of meeting halls.

Maud, he said, shall I see if there's a Gospel Hall near that place you've moved to?

There is, I said, I pass it on the way to work, and I smiled, in a kindly way, to cover the burst of irritation and faint panic that still rises in me twenty years on each time the conversation edges in the direction of my soul.

And now he's been called home. Called as he waited for the sound of the trumpets and the sight of the heavens opening, his little while turning out to be so very long.

He wanted so much to be there around the throne, and yet he was the last to go, outstaying my mother, my father and Aunt Esther by whose graves his own lies now freshly covered in thick yellowy earth and a carpet of flowers.

Among the wreaths I can see one from Matthew, away on business and unable to attend the funeral. He sent a wreath, as he did when Aunt Esther died, as you do when you're chairman of the parish council and the village's most loved and respected son.

The wreath says, 'From Matthew and Mary and the Children', the children, two bright, good-looking teenagers who danced past Uncle Ezra's shuffling figure a hundred times, scarcely knowing who he was.

Time passes, times change. Dozens of villagers turned up to pay their last respects at my mother's funeral but for Uncle Ezra there was just the postman, the woman who did his washing, the man who did the garden and the shopkeeper who stands slicing up the ham and cheese in the spot where once Uncle Ezra stood.

Still, none the less, few as we were, Cousin Arthur sought our souls as Uncle Ezra had done before him. Yes, of course, who but Cousin Arthur, grey-haired now, but still robust and handsome, looking rather like Uncle Ezra, especially when he leant out over us from the pulpit, pleading with us to be saved.

Cousin Arthur turned his yearning eyes on us. But they did not frighten me this time, these eyes less bright and blue it seems to me than before, staring out from the pulpit, just a pulpit now, a huge dark watchtower no longer, in an old Gospel Hall so much smaller than I remember, so much chillier, so much more the worse for wear.

Even the text above his head seemed somehow to have faded both in colour and tone as if 'Except a man be born again', no longer had its old, hard, inflexible ring but was more a suggestion, an idea, the opening gambit in the argument.

Later, after the brief service at the graveside, I shook hands with Cousin Arthur, a quick, cool, polite handshake, of one adult to another.

We asked, courteously, after each other and then he looked at the sky, saying he was glad the rain had held off. He did not tell me, Only a little while, Maud.

I shook hands too with John, a grown-up John with a handsome man's face under fair hair still bright and with a handsome, dark-haired wife by his side. I enquired after their children and we exchanged gentle, meaningless pleasantries.

115

And now everyone has gone and I am alone, sitting upon the old wooden bench seat in the churchyard with their graves before me.

I close my eyes in the warm sunshine, and drift off into dreams, remembering so many things. Somewhere a tractor phut-phuts and a cow lows. A breeze rustles the long church-yard grass and shushes in the trees. It is so quiet, so very quiet, as if I and everything about me are waiting.

And then it comes, breaking the silence, a sweet, soft sound, rising and falling, a whisper at first but then growing strong, gaining confidence – a voice, singing.

The sound weaves around me like a spell, enchanting me. It is in my head, in my ears, in my eyes, catching my breath with its simple melody, tearing my heart with the sad sweetness of its words.

It is me, Maud, singing, singing with a terrible yearning old words, plain words, foolish words, words escaping now, unprompted, unbidden and unstoppable from an old store, long forgotten inside me.

Whiter than the snow
Whiter than the snow
Wash me in the blood of the Lamb
And I shall be whiter than the snow

The words float out into the air with quiet passion. My head moves from side to side as I sing. I lift my chin and close my eyes. I feel tears wet on my cheeks.

Something is breaking out from me. Something is forcing its way up, some strange, sweet, elusive yearning is rising up inside me and speaking of something that won't be denied, that won't be papered over by the years or tidied away by time.

The sound of a step upon the flagged churchyard path and a low cough makes me open my eyes. John is standing above me, his Bible clutched in readiness between his hands.

I lowered my head abruptly, fumbling for a handkerchief with one hand and brushing away tears from my face with an irritated gesture with the other.

Are you all right, Maud? he says.

Raising my head I see on his face the old look of hunger and anticipation before the sight of a soul in distress that I used to see on Uncle Ezra's face as he watched them stumble from their seat to the front at the evangelist's meeting.

I know what John wants. I know what John hopes for. John scents the sweet smell of my soul.

Would you like me to pray with you? he asks.

For a moment, just for a moment, everything seems to stand still. The question hangs upon the air as another question did once before. I wait, as I waited then, for an answer.

It comes in a hiss, in a great intake of breath as my body writhes forward at him in a spasm of anger, horror and revulsion.

It is a No, drawn in through gritted teeth and spat out at him.

He steps back sharply, shock upon his face, as if the No had slapped him. As he does so his Bible drops from his grip, fanning out on to the path texts and pieces of paper. He drops down to one knee scrabbling around on the stone to push them back between the leaves.

The light breeze suddenly lifts a cardboard cross of dark blue edged in gold beyond his grasp and flutters it to my feet. I reach down and pick it up, turning it round, like a windmill, in my hand.

I'm sorry, I say, I didn't mean to be rude.

Before me, John rises to his feet. The look of shock and alarm has faded now and in its place is an expression of hurt that I recognize from a long time ago and which makes him look like a young man again.

I'm sorry, I say again. You caught me at a bad moment, that's all.

Here, I say, Take your cross, and I hand it to him.

He raises a hand towards it, but then drops it.

Keep it, he says, to remind you . . . to help you remember. I look at him questioningly and he becomes bolder. To make you think, he says.

The look of hurt has gone now, edged out by the returning

117

hunger and anticipation. He has recovered his composure and has taken a minute step towards me.

Thank you, I say, dropping it briskly into my large, open bag. Then I glance at my watch and click my teeth ostentatiously over the time, rise to my feet and hold out my hand.

I must fly, I say. And then I am gone, down the path, under the lych gate and into the car with the grip of his hand still tingling on mine.

*

The cardboard cross is like one Uncle Ezra once sent me for Christmas. For a while it amused me to use it as a bookmark in utterly unsuitable books but then, after a while, I tore it up.

But I did not tear up this one, this one that John gave me. I have it now before me. It lies bright blue and gold upon the white of the table.

I have it before me but in truth I do not need his cross to remind me, to help me think, to make me remember. I do not need it for two lines innocently intersecting upon a page do all this for me, plunging me down through layer upon layer of memories and images and dark emotions that together now make up the shadowy Golgotha on which my cross now stands.

Show me a cross and I'll show you humiliation around a camp fire, disappointment on a river bank, pain and confusion at a graveside.

Show me a cross and I'll show you an old woman dreaming, damp-eyed in a pew, an old man dreaming, even when dying, of saving souls.

Show me a cross and I'll show you a mother speechless from fear, a father speechless from love, a daughter speechless with the horror of it all.

Show me a cross and I'll feel again the waters close over my face, washing away the dark emotions to leave in their place the dreadful yearning that came upon me in the churchyard.

It tears at my heart, this yearning. It is elusive and mysterious and melancholy. It will not stop to be examined but fades away almost before it has begun.

118

It belongs to the memory of the words sung sweet and low and passionate with eyes closed and head thrown back.

It belongs to the preacher leaning across me with his arms open wide, his eyes gazing full into mine, urgent and pleading.

It belongs to the handshakes and the stares and to the warm tide of care for my soul that washed over me as I sat beneath the pulpit, that would have choked me and drowned me.

But most of all it belongs to the stranger, the blue-robed, golden-faced stranger, who stands in the light of his lantern and knocks in tyrannous love forever upon the door of my heart.

*

Here I am then, outside the wedding hall, this virgin, most foolish of all.

Here I am then in the ragged old bridesmaid's dress, my lamp gone cold in my hand.

From the hall I can hear feasting and dancing, the sound of the pipes and the tabors, the sound of laughing.

Sometimes I think I hear the sound of the Bridegroom's voice and when I do I rise to my feet and rap on the door but nobody answers.

And so I sit down again on the steps and I wait and, waiting, I polish my lamp on my skirt. I rub till it shines, till it gleams like a mirror, till I can look into its heart and see my own face. I smile and it smiles, a smile as gentle and rueful as mine. I stare into the lamp and I smile and I say, Only a little while, Maud, only a little while.